Loving You Is A Battle 2

Tina J

Copyright 2019

More books from me:

The Thug I Chose 1, 2 & 3

A Thin Line Between Me and My Thug 1 & 2

I Got Luv For My Shawty 1 & 2

Kharis and Caleb: A Different Kind of Love 1 & 2

Loving You Is A Battle 1 & 2 & 3

Violet and The Connect 1 & 2 & 3

You Complete Me

Love Will Lead You Back

This Thing Called Love

Are We In This Together 1,2 &3

Shawty Down To Ride For a Boss 1, 2 &3

When A Boss Falls in Love 1, 2 & 3

Let Me Be The One 1 & 2

We Got That Forever Love

Aint No Savage Like The One I Got 1&2

A Queen and A Hustla 1, 2 & 3

Thirsty For A Bad Boy 1&2

Hassan and Serena: An Unforgettable Love 1&2

My Brother's Keeper 1. 2 & 3

C'Yani & Meek: A Dangerous Hood Love 1, 2 & 3

When A Savage Falls for A Good Girl 1, 2 & 3

Eva & Deray 1 & 2

Blame It On His Gangsta Luv 1 & 2

Falling for The Wrong Hustla 1, 2 & 3

I Gave My Heart to A Jersey Killa 1, 2 & 3

Luvin The Son of a Savage 1, 2 & 3

A Dopeman and His Shawty 1, 2 & 3

Darius

I had been at my office for hours going over the video footage from the club when Mike walked in looking suspect as usual. He looked around my office like he never been in there before. I leaned back in my chair and folded my hands on my stomach. After about a minute I thought this nigga didn't see me until he spoke.

"Yo D have you ever thought about getting a exit door that leads outside in here?" Louis walked in and sat on the edge of my desk. He picked up a piece of candy I had and put it in his mouth.

"Louis did you hear what Mike just asked me?"

"Nah. What's up Mike?"

"He asked if I thought about having an exit door in my office?" Louis looked him up and down and frowned his face up.

"Why would he need that when you're the one protecting us? Nobody should be able to pass the steps with you standing there."

"Yea I guess you can look at it like that."

"Mike let me ask you something?" I stood up to close the door.

"Sure boss."

"Have a seat. Make yourself comfortable."

"Ok. But I have to get back downstairs to watch the door."

"Don't worry about that because Amir is covering your post. See." I turned my monitor all the way around so he could see.

"Oh. I didn't know he was here." He started shifting in his chair. Louis was now sitting on my desk with his legs hanging off playing with his gun.

"I have two questions for you and I expect you to keep it 100."

"Ok." I could see Cream coming in the club. He locked the front door and said something to Amir on his way up. He stepped in and closed the door.

"See we took you in when you were just a snot nose kid and let you make so much money your kids would never have to work. What I don't understand is how a nigga can not only bite the hand that feeds him but chew that shit off."

"Huh? I don't know what you're talking about."

"Alright, lets start here then." Cream walked over showing a video of him and Kelly fucking in his truck.

"She said you two weren't fucking around anymore."

"It doesn't matter what she told you it's all about respect. You were supposed to be my boy and my boys wouldn't do that."

"Some shit just aint adding up bro." I looked back at Cream.

"You see the day that nigga Monster put a bomb in my car you came out behind me and my girl as if you were waiting for it to go off."

"No. I was checking the building." Louis was tying his arms behind his back on the chair.

"You're going to have to come better than that. Who the fuck is this dude to you and what does he want?" He knew he was caught so he put his head down in defeat.

"That's my cousin. I don't know what he wants."

"Louis stuck a knife in the top of his leg." Now usually I'm not into torturing but he's the closet thing to this nigga.

"Ok. Ok. He doesn't like your girl and because CiCi is her sister he wants both of them. I don't know why but he hates Iesha. He plans on taking over your operation and this club. "

"Is that why you came in eye my office? Did that nigga promise you an office?"

"Yes."

"Right answer. Now tell me. Did you take these pictures and what do they mean?" He shook his head yes. Louis was laying a blue tarp around his chair.

"If you look in each picture Iesha and CiCi are in them."

"Where? I've looked over these photos a million times." I handed them to him and if you look closely they were in front of me in the pictures. You wouldn't know unless you knew the clothes they wore because that's all that was visible. He made sure not to put their faces in them.

"I'm going to give you a chance to save your life." His eyes grew big when I said that.

"I'll tell you what you want to know."

"Tell us everything that you were involved in and how this all comes together."

"He started running his mouth and to say we were taken aback was not even the word. This nigga was working with Kelly to make CiCi lose every baby she became pregnant with. He told her CiCi's every move. The last straw was when he told her that Iesha was in the room alone because I was in with Lyric. He knew all this stuff because he was always right there. Here he was pretending to protect us when the whole time he was in on the plan.

"One more question and then we'll decide if you can live." He now had tears running down his face. The fear on his face was evident.

"When is this nigga supposed to touch soil in Jersey?"

"He's already here."

"Thanks?" Cream shot him in the head and pressed the intercom for them to send the clean up crew to do their job.

I picked the phone up and dialed the number of the person I needed to see. He answered on the third ring.

"What up?"

"Yo Monster guess who?"

"Who is this?"

"Don't tell me you forgot my voice. Come on. I'm offended."

"I don't have time for games. Who the fuck is this?"

"This is your worst fucking nightmare nigga."

"Ahhh this is my friend who has my merchandise."

"Yup. That's me."

"Don't worry I've got my people keeping my eyes on it. Plus, I have eyes on you too."

"Oh I'm sorry to inform you but your eyes is lying on the middle of my floor with a bullet to the head. I don't think he'll be waking up anytime soon but hey that's what happens when you send a boy to do a man's job." The phone went silent.

"Oh don't tell me you're upset."

"When I catch you I'm going to choke the life out of you for killing my cousin."

"Oh, so now that we're on the same page I heard you touched ground in my area. What's up? You ready for the meet and greet or what?"

"You think you're funny nigga but I'm already about to meet and greet with my merchandise. I'm pulling up right now."

"You outside my establishment nigga." I pulled the cameras up. There was no one outside.

"Nah, but I'm pulling up to your motherfucking house."

"Yea right." I heard him ring a doorbell.

"Monster." I heard Iesha's voice and the phone went dead.

Iesha

I had just turned the shower water off when I heard the doorbell ring. I wasn't expecting anyone and the nanny Darius made me hire, took Summer for a walk. He wanted us to stay with him until he found out who was sending him death threats. If you ask me, he already knows but won't disclose that information with me.

I threw his robe on because it was thicker and longer. I didn't have time to get dressed due to the person at the door. I opened it and was surprised as hell to see who it was.

"Monster!" I yelled out. He closed his phone up and tried to step inside.

"Ugh, I think not nigga." I pushed his ass back and stood there with my arms folded. He still looked good as hell standing there with his fresh shave, dreads neatly hanging down his back, jeans, a t-shirt and some Giuseppe sneakers. His diamond necklace and earrings topped the entire out off. I couldn't help but lick my lips.

"I see you like what you see." He said grinning. This

man used to be my weakness until I went to visit him and tried to take his life.

"Ci, I'm about to head to Phila now to see Monster. I'll call you when I get there."

"Be safe Esh. You know I hate when you drive down there at night. Why can't his ass come up here?"

"Ci come on we've been over this. You know we take turns visiting each other. I'm going to move down there soon and it'll be you and me taking the trips to visit one another." I told her getting in my car.

"Yea I know. Ok call me as soon as you get there." We gave each other a hug and I got in the car and left.

I picked my phone up and called Monster to tell him I was on the way but as usual he didn't answer. This was nothing new for him; I figured he was playing that stupid ass game with one of his boys; most likely Jermaine. I turned on my old school Mary J Blige and cruised down there.

I finally got there around nine from getting caught in the rush hour traffic leaving Jersey.

I opened the door with my set of keys and headed for

the basement where he probably was. I left my luggage in the car because it was dark out and I was not getting my shit stolen. His ass did not live in the best of neighborhoods. That's why the house we looked out was in the suburbs. Shit; he can visit his friends out here but living here is no longer an option. Call me bossy all you want.

I made it to the basement where it sounded like I was hearing grunting. I got to the bottom of the steps and didn't see anyone; but the smell of weed was in the air and music was playing. He had two rooms down there with a bathroom.

The first room I checked had me in total disbelief. I stood there with tears streaming down my face as I watched my future husband giving some man my dick.

I backed up quietly, grabbed a knife from the kitchen, and stabbed that nigga five times. I didn't even stay to watch his body drop. I hopped in my car, drove back to Jersey and never spoke of the shit to anyone. I was more embarrassed then anything, so I stayed in a hotel instead of going home. I went back to my house the next day and told Ci Ci I caught him cheating. Now I'm sitting here with him looking good as ever on my doorstep; well Darius doorstep.

"You wish Monster. What are you doing here?" I asked looking over his shoulder and seeing some guy waiting in the car.

"I came to see my ex fiancé. I know you missed me." He took his hand and ran it inside my robe and let it stop on my pussy.

"Boy back up. Don't come over here on no disrespectful shit." I yelled smacking his hand away.

"I see she still gets wet at the sight of me." I smirked because he was right. My kitty was wet the moment I laid eyes on him. Gay or not, his swag stayed on point.

"Whatever. What do you want?" I asked closing my robe tighter.

"Can we talk?"

"Not here. This is my man's house and you showing up here is disrespectful as fuck."

"How about I leave you my number. You can call me when he doesn't have you on a leash."

"Negro please. No man has ever had me on one; you

should know that by now." I told him. He placed a piece of paper in the pocket of the robe and walked away. I stood there for a minute watching him.

When he got in the car he winked and chucked up the deuces. I shut the door and ran upstairs to get dressed. I had to tell Ci Ci what happened. I picked my phone up and I had over 30 missed calls from Darius.

"Iesha please tell me you're ok."

"Yes Darius. I'm fine. What's wrong with you? Why do you sound like that?" I asked while I was putting clothes on.

"Where are you?"

"I'm at your house." I told him still putting on my clothes.

"I'll be there in 30 seconds." I hung the phone up. I remembered the paper Monster gave mem put his number in my phone before I flushed it down the toilet. I don't know why I was hiding it; I just didn't want any shit.

I was walking downstairs when Darius, Cream, Louis and a few other dudes came in searching the house.

"What the hell is going on?"

"Where is he?"

"Where is who? Darius what is going on?" I was getting pissed that they were running through the house like the FBI raiding someone shit.

"Monster."

"Monster?" I questioned. Why was he looking for my ex?

"Yea Monster."

"How do you know him?" I asked.

"Fuck all the questions. Where is he?" He towered over ice grilling me.

"He's not here."

"Where did he go?"

"What the hell is going on? And don't make me ask again." Iesha that's the nigga whose been sending the death threats, placing bombs under my car and was just on the phone talking shit. I heard when he rang the doorbell and you answered.

"Yea he was here but he didn't say anything about looking for you. He claimed he came by to talk to me."

19

"Is that all he said."

"Yea."

"Iesha, I'm only going to ask you one time. Are you fucking that nigga?" I wanted to smack him across the face, but I held back.

"Are you serious right now? Hell no I'm not sleeping with him. When would I have the chance? Do you think I'm a trifling bitch like that?" He tried to hug me and I pushed him away.

"Iesha, my bad. I just need to know how you affiliated with him?"

"Why?" I didn't want to mention how I knew him.

"He called me talking about I have his merchandise and it needs to be returned and then he shows up at my motherfucking doorstep. How the hell does he know you?" I blew my breath and crossed my arms. I saw the way Cream and Louis stared at me like they were waiting for an answer to.

"Monster is my ex fiancé." All of their mouths dropped to the floor. I sat on the couch staring out the window explaining why we broke up.

"No shit. So you're the one who tried to kill him?" Cream said shaking his head laughing.

"Yup, and I'm not ashamed to admit it. You play with my heart and I'll kill you; well at least try. I did think he was dead until the news reported a possible home invasion. Can you believe that nigga never told on me? I haven't heard from him in years and then he just show up on the doorstep." I saw Darius rubbing his head.

"You still feeling that nigga Iesha?" He caught me by surprise with that statement.

"I'm going to pretend you didn't just ask me that asinine question." I tried to push passed him but he grabbed my arm and held it tight.

"Nah, you're going to answer that shit."

"What Darius?"

"You heard me. Are you feeling him?" I looked him in his face and lied.

"No." I didn't know what I was feeling at the moment.

Monster was looking fresh to death and he did get my pussy wet. I had different thoughts running through my mind.

21

Did I still love him? Was I feeling him? Do I want to be with him? The only way I would know is if I met up with him. I needed to see what he was here for anyway and if he did try and kill me.

Darius let my arm go but I know him. He wasn't going to leave it alone; but for now he would because his brother and Louis was here. I know this was a storm brewing; it's probably better if I go back to my own house until this shit with them blows over.

CiCi

I called Cream to find out where he was to see if he could pick me up some Popeye's. I was fiending for some of their mashed potatoes and that spicy chicken sandwich.

He came in an hour later, dropped my food off and went upstairs to take a shower. I was feeling some type of way because he always kissed me before he did anything.

"Baby what's wrong?" I asked him standing outside the bathroom stuffing my face.

"Nothing why?" He slid the curtain back to speak.

"I didn't get my kiss and you didn't even say hello."

"Oh shit, come here baby. Let me show you how much I missed you." He came out the shower-soaking wet, put my food on the nightstand, threw me on the bed and climbed on top of me.

"James, I just took a shower. Come on, you're getting me wet."

"Let me find out you don't want your husband." I felt bad after whining.

"You know I want you." I took my pajama top off and pushed his head into my chest. He knew that was one of my spots and he loved sucking on them. His hands went into my pants and as he was sticking his fingers in, the doorbell rang.

"Ugh uh baby keep going." I moaned in his ear. We tried to get into, but the person was persistent.

"Get the door baby. We got all night." He said going back to the shower.

"James." He turned around. I walked over to him, squatted down and put his dick in my mouth.

"Oh shit Ci Ci." He guided my head up and down. The person was now banging on the door.

"Gettttt the doorrrrr baby." His ass was stuttering. I jerked him faster as I slobbed and sucked.

"Don't stop. Fuck the door."

"You like it baby." I stared up at him.

"I love it baby. I'm about to cum. Shit. Fuckkkkkk. Awwww suck that shit baby." I made sure all his babies were in my mouth. I stood up, wiped my mouth and kissed him.

"You the shit Ci. I love you."

"I love you too. Let me get this door." I went downstairs without even looking at the monitors and snatched the door open.

"WHAT?????" I yelled out.

"Damn bitch, took you long enough." Iesha said rushing past me with Summer.

"Bitch, I was sucking my husband's dick. You know we relieve each other's stress when we get home."

"Ok, I didn't need to know that. But since I do, you might want to go rinse your mouth and shit before you finish talking."

"Why. I love it just like that." James said coming down the steps.

"Well I don't need your dick on her breath while we talk and Summer don't want it on her cheeks."

25

"Whatever. I'll be right back." I went upstairs to brush my teeth and wash my face. I gargled with a little mouthwash too before I went back down there. I saw James holding Summer and Iesha yelling on the phone. He looked at me shaking his head.

"Here baby take Summer. I'm going upstairs to watch TV. You know what I want when she leaves right?" He whispered in my ear making me smile.

"Maybe. Maybe not."

"Stop playing Ci Ci or you won't get this tongue."

"Ok damn. I'll be up there shortly." He grinned and ran up the steps. I grabbed Summer from her and sat down. She started telling me about how her ex Monster came to the house a last week and he was the one trying to kill them. I was shocked he would try and kill her after all the years they were together.

"But why would he try to kill you? And why did it take you a week to tell me?"

"Ci there's something I never told you or anyone for that matter." She went on to tell me how she caught him with

26

another man and she stabbed him five times. I covered my mouth and sat there in complete shock.

"What happened when he stopped by the house?" She told me what happened.

"Esh, please tell me you're not thinking about calling him."

"He just wants to talk and I need to know why he's trying to kill us."

"Esh, I'm your sister and I'm telling you this is a bad idea. You think he means well but he came back here for a reason."

"Ci, I know Monster and whatever the reason is I want to know. What's the harm in meeting him in a public place?"

"Would you want Darius to meet someone he used to fuck or almost married to in a public place?"

"It doesn't matter what I wanted; he met her in an office and had a baby with her. What's the difference?"

"That's different because you forgave him for it and accepted Lyric as your step daughter." I was trying to talk sense into her but she wouldn't listen.

"Ci, I already text and told him I would meet him tomorrow for lunch." I rolled my eyes. I knew it was a bad idea.

"Esh, you're my sister and I love you. I'm going to have your back no matter what but just listen to me. Darius loves you and would move buildings just to keep you safe. At least tell him what you're planning so he can keep an eye on you."

"What? He is not going to be ok with this at all. That's why I'm not saying a word."

"At least text me where you'll be in case something happens."

"I will." She stayed over a little longer and told me she was going back to her place because her and Darius needed a break. If I know my sister, she is going to do what she wanted.

"Bring that sexy ass here." My husband said when I walked in the bedroom. I stripped then crawled on the bed to him. He tossed the remote on the nightstand and pulled my face to his.

"I love you James."

"I love you too baby. What's wrong?" I sat on top of him naked.

I was so in love with this man; I couldn't imagine one of his ex's coming back and trying to take him out to eat. I told him what my sister and I talked about.

"I know you wanna help but your sister is her own person and she's going to do what she wants. He was pulling his boxers down while he spoke.

"You're righttttttttt." I moaned out as he entered me. His size felt like it ripped me open every time and I loved it.

"Shit James I'm going to cum already." I told him going up and down. After I came, he climbed on top of me. He took long deep strokes and stared into my eyes as he made love to me.

"Ci Ci."

"Yes baby. Oh God it feels so good." I couldn't help moaning.

"I want you to have another baby." I let a few tears drop. He leaned down and kissed them away.

"Of course baby. I'll have as many kids as you want. Shittttt I'm cumming." My legs started shaking.

"I love you Ci Ci. Don't you ever forget that?" He came inside me over and over and I let him. If he wanted a bunch of babies, I was the only one giving them to him.

Cream

Ci Ci was my soul mate in every way possible. No other woman was going to make me feel as complete as she does. This woman stayed on my mind from the moment I woke up, until the moment I went to bed. I would never allow any harm come to her.

Unfortunately, I did something so foul that may cost her; her life and freedom.

I looked down at my wife as she slept peacefully after I made love to her. My phone buzzed and I knew who it was; I just didn't want to look at it.

Unknown: *Same place tomorrow*? Is what the text read? I didn't wanna respond. I was faced with two choices and that was continuing this charade or allow my wife to face life in prison for murder. I ran my hand down my face and responded.

Me: *"Yea a'ight."* I put my phone down and laid back with my hands behind my head.

I woke up the next day tired as hell. I finally dosed off after three and I'm up again at seven. I had to meet this person at ten and hopefully I would be back in my office by twelve. I parked in the driveway and walked to the door.

"Well hello. You don't look happy to see me." I pushed past and went straight to the bar area to get a drink.

"It's a little early to be drinking, don't you think?"

"Don't worry about what I'm doing. Let's just get this over with so I can leave."

I went to use the bathroom before I had to do this shit. I flushed, washed my hands and glanced in the mirror. *What the fuck am I doing? This is going to kill my wife.* I thought to myself before I opened the door.

I was pushed against the wall when I came out and my pants and boxers hit my ankles in seconds. She took my dick in her mouth and sucked me off until I came. She stood up and bent over in front of me. Her ass was huge and even though that's not the type of women I'm into, I have to admit, the shit turned me on and had me at attention. I entered her and she jumped forward.

"Ok, then what."

"What do you mean, then what?"

"She was still ass naked. Why didn't you send her ass home and go tell CiCi? Better yet, all you had to do was pick the phone up and call Miguel."

"I know D but I wasn't thinking. I would never allow my wife or any of the girls to go to jail."

"So you fucked her?"

"Yea, I fucked her. At first it started out as that one time but in the last two weeks she has wanted the shit every day just about. When I tell her no, she starts talking about showing the DA the video and I give in."

"What happened today?"

"She text me in the middle of the night. Thank goodness my wife was asleep. I don't know what to do."

"Miguel can handle it without you getting your hands dirty."

"I know man but what the fuck am I going to do about this? Ci Ci and I have sex just about every night. We shower together and I never sleep in anything but my boxers."

"Pick a fight with her."

"Huh? We never had an argument since we've been together except when she got arrested and even then, she just stopped speaking to me. Man, I fucked up."

"I don't even know what to say. You can go home when you think she's asleep, then fuck her and make her think she left it."

"That's crazy man. But it may work." I can't believe I'm even entertaining this shit.

"Hey, I'm trying to help you out." He gave me a pound and stepped out. I called Ci Ci and told her I was working late and not to wait up for me. She was ok with that because she knows I wanted to keep an eye on the staff every now and then.

I left the club a little after one because I knew she was asleep. I jumped in the shower and got in bed with her. I rubbed my fingers in between her legs and felt her moaning a little in my sleep.

When I could tell she was awake, I rolled her on top of me. She loved pleasing me orally and I knew she would suck on my chest. Bingo, that's exactly what she did first before handling her business.

The next morning, I got in the shower behind her. She turned around and wrapped her arms around my neck.

"Damn baby I didn't know I sucked that hard on you." She pointed to the mark on my chest. I felt like shit but I went along with it. I had to make that call to my cousin and fast. This shit was getting out of control.

Monster

The day I stopped by that nigga's house and saw my ex, all my emotions came back. Iesha was supposed to be my wife and we're supposed to be happily married by now. Seeing her standing there in just a robe had my dick hard. I knew I still had an effect on her when I felt her pussy and it was wet. She tried to play it off like I didn't get to her but I beg to differ.

When she caught me in the compromising position with the guy that was the first time. Grant it; Jermaine and I were both fucked up and he sucked my dick better than a bitch. He wanted me to fuck him and since I already let him suck me off, I figured why not; I fuck chicks in the ass all the time; couldn't be much different than that. And it wasn't.

It was tight like a female and I didn't touch his dick. Iesha stabbed me but I wasn't even mad at her. I understood why she did it. I wish she let me explain before she did it and we probably could've moved past it.

I'm not going to lie, I thought maybe I was gay myself. Jermaine wanted me to fuck him again and being the selfish nigga I was, I allowed him to suck my dick more then I fucked him.

After a few more times he wanted me to be his man and come out. That wasn't happening because I still loved pussy and my fiancé, Iesha's at that. It took me a few months to get myself together and when I didn't hear from her, I let her be.

Low and behold, my cousin Mike was calling me complaining about these two niggas he fucked with who were getting money. Unfortunately, Mike was in his feelings because he started fucking one of the boss's ex-girlfriends. You know you get salty when the new chick you hitting off still stuck on her old nigga.

Imagine my surprise when I found out his bosses were the ones that ran guns up and down the East Coast and his cousin was the motherfucking Connect. Once he told me they fucked with some sisters and gave me their names, I thought it was fate. I set up a brilliant plan to take them out but my dumb ass cousin fucked that up and got himself killed.

I had just come back from P.R meeting with this shiesty ass bitch Faith who used to date the Connect but he dumped her. Now she and I were about to get his ass for all his money. She showed me a photo of his girl and told me she left him and was out here in Jersey with her family visiting and she wanted to get at her. I told her I'll think about helping her. The bitch ain't the one with the money.

Today I was meeting up with Iesha and then, tonight I was headed out to some club this chick was supposed to be at.

"You look sexy as hell Iesha." I told her kissing her cheek. We were in the restaurant in the hotel I was staying at. She wore a brown romper with some strap up heels. Her hair and make-up was always done and her perfume invaded my nostrils.

"Thanks Monster. What's up?" We sat down and ordered our food.

"Tell me why you tried to kill me and my man." She was straight to the point.

"To be honest, I was only after your man, but you happened to be in the wrong place at the wrong time."

"Ok, why are you after my man?"

"Come on Iesha. You know we're all in the same game. Every man wants to be at the top and sometimes we have to do crazy shit to get there."

"Monster, I just want you to stop going after him. I love him and as far as your merchandise. Hold the fuck up." She said putting her finger up. I looked over at what she was seeing and it was her sisters' husband coming off the elevator with a fly ass chic. She was rubbing on his chest and kissing him. You can tell they just fucked.

"Oh shit. It looks like somebody is being a naughty boy." I said. She picked her phone up and snapped a ton of photos and then videotaped him put her in the car and kiss her.

"Iesha don't get involved. That's your sisters' shit."

"Hell no. This motherfucker portrays himself to be Mr. goody two shoes and he out here cheating on my sister."

"I need you to come to my room. I have something to show you." I told her after we finished eating.

"Yea right nigga. Whom do you take me for?"

"Fine. I just want us to talk in a more private spot. I want to tell you what really happened that night you almost

43

killed me." I didn't think she would, but I guess she felt she owed me that much.

"This room is nice Monster." She walked around looking.

"Hell yea. You know I sleep in the best."

"Please. You stayed in the hood in Phila."

"Yea but my shit was laced." She waved me off.

"What are you going to do with those pictures and photos?" I was talking about the ones she took on her phone.

"I'm gonna send them to my sister. I love Cream like my own brother, but I'll be damned if he plays my sister out for some trick."

"You don't know if she's a trick."

"Oh that bitch's a trick. I saw his ring on, which means she knows he's married."

"Come here girl." I sat her on my lap. She tried to push herself up but I held her down.

"Listen, what you saw back then was a mistake." I explained to her what happened and she looked shocked.

"Monster if you were bisexual you should've told me that."

"That's just it, I'm not. After I told him to beat it I never did it again. Iesha you are the only woman I ever loved. I came back for you because I love you and now you're with that fuck nigga who had a baby on you." I saw she was struggling with her thoughts. I moved her head towards mine and parted her lips with my tongue. She accepted it and kissed me back aggressively.

"Mmmmm Iesha. I miss you girl."

"Shit, Monster. I missed you too but I'm with Darius now." She told me. I pulled her romper down and sucked on her chest. I fell back on the bed and she fell on top of me. She stood up taking her clothes off and pulled my clothes down. I stood at attention and let her slide down. Her pussy felt the same as when she left me.

"Shit Jeremy. I still love this dick." I loved when she called me by my real name.

"Iesha, I'm going to cum. Turn over." I beat that pussy up. She and I fucked like she didn't have a man at home. I walked her downstairs and to her car.

"Ok Iesha. This is what you wanted right?" Her man called out to her. She looked petrified.

"Darius."

"Yea Darius bitch."

"Yo man don't call her a bitch."

"Shut your bitch ass up. Iesha, I asked you if you were feeling this nigga and you told me no. Its mighty funny how you're coming out of a hotel with him. Your hair is fucked up, clothes wrinkled. I mean it's clear you fucked him." It wasn't shit Iesha could say. She just got in her car and pulled off.

"It's me and you nigga. What's up?"

"I'm not about to fight you over no chick that clearly doesn't want you." This nigga swung off and we were going at it until security broke us up.

"I'll see you around my nigga." I told him. I went back to my room to get ready for my date at the club. That nigga will have his day.

Darius

I was calling Iesha's phone all afternoon, but she didn't answer. I was worried because the nigga was in town and I thought he did something to her. I tracked her phone to some hotel and there she was coming out looking like she just got fucked.

I couldn't believe she did a nigga like that but it was my fault for not paying closer attention. I saw the look in her eye the day he left the house. I could tell she was feeling him but no; I went by what she said and look where it got me. I got to her house and used my key to go inside.

"Iesha." I heard the shower water running.

"Don't try and wash his scent off you now. I know you fucked him." I pulled the curtain back and she had two hickeys on her neck. I wanted to yank her dumb ass out but I closed the curtain back and walked out.

"Darius wait."

"Wait for what?"

"Darius, I just met him for lunch and we went to his room to talk and then one thing led to another."

"I know it just happened. No one knew his dick would end up in your pussy right?"

"Darius please."

"Please what Iesha?" I was yelling in her face.

"Just listen."

"Nah, I've done enough listening to you. Was this your payback for me fucking Sky and having a baby with her?" She didn't answer.

"WAS IT?"

"I love you Darius." I laughed in her face.

"Iesha, we weren't even fighting, arguing or anything and you fucked him. I could see if we were going through something, but we weren't. You did what you did because its what you wanted. You have never been the one to allow someone to tell you what to do."

"That's not true."

"Yes it is and you know it. Here I am feeling bad every day about the shit I did with Sky when you broke up with me.

48

But you fucking niggas like it's a sport and we together. Where they do that shit at?"

"Like a sport. Nigga this is the first time I cheated on you. Don't make it seem like I do this shit all the time."

"Answer me this Iesha. When did you get his number?"

"The day he came here."

"How many times have you spoken to him since then?"

She put her head down.

"HOW MANY?"

"Every day."

"Exactly. Just because you didn't fuck him until today; you still entertained the nigga. You allowed him to get up in your head. Any conversation was better than no conversation with him. That nigga came back for you. He came back for you Iesha and you went to him." I felt myself getting upset. I loved the hell out of her and she did me dirty for the next nigga.

"Darius, I didn't go to him."

"Oh no. Then why does he think you're seeing him tomorrow." I lifted up her phone and showed her the message that said he would see her tomorrow.

49

"You going through my phone now?"

"Nah, baby girl. You left it open and it popped up. But it's all-good. I'm out."

"Oh so you're just going to leave? I took you back after you had a baby on me."

"Yea, and we were broken up when it happened. You took me back and I told you I would never accept that baby if you didn't. You told me you would and never left me. I loved you even more after that day but you fucked up. Ain't no way in hell I'm fucking you after him or any other nigga for that matter. Your pussy is tainted."

"Tainted. Was it tainted when you were in it this morning?" I hemmed her ass up on the wall.

"No because you weren't touched yet. That makes the shit worse because you fucked two niggas in one day. Only ho's do shit like that. But you can have all the memories of our sex life because you and I will only speak on the strength of my daughter; who I'm taking home with me tonight." I chucked up the deuces and walked out.

I heard her let out a gut-wrenching scream, but I didn't give two shits. That bitch had me twisted if she thought I was fucking her again.

I walked in my house and forgot I left Sky and Lyric there to check on Iesha. I had nothing to hide and she had been to the house plenty of times Iesha wasn't there. We both knew there would never be an us and we stayed friends.

Sky came and took Summer out my arms and put her in the playpen with her sister. I took my jacket off and called up a locksmith. I told him I would pay double if they could get out to my house tonight. I didn't want that bitch having a key to any of my shit.

"Is everything ok D?" Sky asked passing me a water bottle.

"Yea, I'm good. You know what Sky. Let me ask you something." She sat at the table with me.

"What's up?" She asked looked down at her phone playing that dumb ass Trivia Crack game.

"Do you think I'm a grimy nigga? I mean, if I made you my girl would you cheat on me?" She put the phone down and looked up at me.

"What's this about?"

"Just answer it please."

"Well Darius, I would never cheat on you because I've always wanted to be with you. I know you believed I was with you just for your money and at first, I was. I can admit that but I fell in love with you as a person. The more we hung out and talked, laughed and just chilled you became more than a fuck buddy and ATM. But you chose another, and I can respect that. I don't think you're a grimy nigga unless you're pushed." I was shocked at her answer. I didn't know she felt that way about me.

"Are you going to explain to me what this is about?"

"No. I just had some random thoughts that's all."

"Ok, well can you tell me why you have a locksmith coming to change your locks this late?"

"Sky it's only six."

52

"Yea but they close at five and you offered to pay double. What's really going on? Are you two fighting?"

"It's a long story and I rather not talk about it. Do you mind staying the night and keeping and eye on the girls? I'm going to run by the club and I'll probably get in late."

"Sure Darius. Whatever is going on between y'all, I'm sure you can work it out. I mean you two love one another."

"Yea, but what if love isn't enough?" I left her money for the locksmith, kissed the girls and left. I needed a drink.

Cream

The day I told my brother what was going on with the detective, I it felt like a weight was lifted. I called my cousin, but he was out of town and told me he would hit me up and soon as he got back.

I could've told him but I didn't want to bother him, I know he was going through some shit with his wife from what Darius told me. I was tired of this back and forth shit with this woman and it was finally taking a toll on me.

Ci Ci was in the bed naked waiting for me to get out the shower. We've been trying for baby number two every day since I said something. It was nothing for me to make love to her but my body was drained from fucking two women at once. That was one of the main reasons I never cheated on my women. I always wanted my dick to be accessible to her without me being tired.

I let the hot water beat down on me as I thought about killing the detective myself.

"Damn baby you trying to kill me?" I asked dropping my towel.

"I'm just trying to make sure my man is happy."

"You make me happy with or without sex. Don't ever doubt yourself when it comes to that."

"I'm not. I just love satisfying you." She stroked my man to get him hard and for some reason it didn't work. I put my head back tryna focus to at least get a semi hard on, but it wasn't working. This was the first time since I've been with her that its happened.

"Are you ok?" She asked me with concerning eyes.

"Yea Ci Ci. I'm just stressed. Get on top, you know that always works." I laid back on the bed and kissed her. She straddled me and tried getting me hard again and nothing. I felt like shit because I knew it was my fault. She rolled off of me and turned on her side.

"Ci Ci don't worry about it."

"Don't worry about it. How can you tell me not to worry about it when I'm trying to make love to my husband and his dick doesn't work? The only reason that happens is if

55

he's sleeping with someone else. I know damn well that's not happening."

"Baby stop, you're thinking too much."

"James, what am I supposed to think? This has never happened with us. What's going on?" I turned her around and saw her crying. I had to get rid of that bitch quick. I couldn't stand seeing my wife like this. I kissed over her body and went to please her and she closed her legs.

"What the fuck Ci Ci?"

"I'm tired."

"You wasn't just tired when you tried to hit me off."

"Well I'm tired now."

"That's bullshit. I'm trying to please my wife and she closes her legs."

"The difference between what I did is that I want you to please me because I know you can but for what? Your dick won't get hard to give me that afterwards so what's the use?"

"Ci Ci stop with the theatrics and open your legs."

"No James. Just go to sleep."

"Hell no. Sit up. We're about to talk about this shit. You and I have never argued since we've been together and the first one is about my dick not getting hard."

"Ok how would you feel if my pussy didn't get wet when you went down on me? Or when you stuck your dick inside, it was like fucking sand paper. Would you be ok with that?" I thought about what she was saying and she was right.

"Ci Ci you're making this more than what it is."

"Just go to bed James. I have to get up early tomorrow."

"I'm good. I think I'll sleep I the guest room and play with my dick."

"Oh, if you think you could get it up better than I could, then be my guest."

"Somebody's going to have to get it up since my wife can't." I knew that was a low blow as soon as I said it. She gasped and covered her mouth with tears running down her face. I didn't even know I could speak to her like that. She didn't deserve that, and I only said it because that bitch was fucking up my marriage.

"Ci Ci."

"No James. Say no more. You said enough."

"I didn't mean it."

"Yes you did. I hate when people say they didn't mean it. If you weren't thinking it; you never would've said it."

"Look, I don't wanna fight with you. Our first argument wasn't supposed to be over something like this."

"Did you expect us to argue over money or other women? Who picks what kind of argument they'll have?"

"I didn't mean it like that."

"James just be honest with me. Is there someone else? Just tell me I can take it." The pain on her face was killing me.

"No baby. I told you I don't cheat on my woman."

"Then I don't know what the problem is."

"I've been stressed at work and we've been trying for a baby that's probably all it is."

"I don't know James. I just want to go to bed. The sheets are clean in the guest room. If you get your dick up, change the sheets please." She said an pulled the covers up. I stormed out the room and plopped down on the guest bed. I put my head in my hands and picked my phone that was buzzing.

Unknown: *I love the way your dick felt inside me today. I can't get enough of you. Can we hook up again tomorrow?* I didn't keep her saved in my phone.

Me: *Where?*

Unknown: *Hotel.* She sent me the address and room number. I tossed the phone on the bed and laid down.

I got up and went to shower in my room. The bed was made and when I looked out the window my wife's car was gone. I left the house a little after nine and went to the hotel. I knocked on the door and she stood there in just a towel. I stepped inside while she shut the door.

"I felt like it took you forever to get here." She said dropping her towel. My dick stood straight up. How in the hell did my dick get up for her and not my wife? Was I falling for her? What the hell was going on? She got down on her knees and sucked me off until I came in her mouth. She scooted back on the bed with her legs gapped open.

"Oh God this feels so good." She said squeezing my dick with her pussy. The orgasm she released was coming out like a waterfall. We left the room and she was rubbing on my chest in the lobby. I tried to move her hand just in case someone saw us. I kissed her when she got in the car and left right behind her.

Ci Ci was at work, so I decided to go home and change my clothes before I went to the club.

Ci Ci

I was a mess going to work today over the shit between my husband and me. I didn't know what was going on but there was definitely a change. I noticed him coming in later and later, and then his phone going off in the middle of the night. It doesn't take a rocket scientist to know someone else is holding his attention. I don't know who she is but I pray to God he wasn't sleeping with her.

I was on my way to the second store I had to visit today when I got a few messages from my sister at once. I should've pulled over to check them because when I opened it, I almost crashed.

I got off the next exit and headed back to my house. I called the manager of the store and told them I had an emergency and would come to their tomorrow. I'm sure they were happy because it gave them more time to clean it up.

I pulled up to my house and parked behind him. What was he doing home this early? I went inside and heard the shower running. I poured me a glass of wine and went upstairs.

"Hello James." I said leaning against the bathroom door. I could tell he was shocked I was home by the way he snatched the curtain back.

"What are you doing here?" He asked. I took a sip before answering.

"Oh, I called out of work."

"Why you do that?" He asked turning the shower off. He stepped out and I handed him a towel.

"Thanks."

"Why aren't you at work yet?" I asked to see what his answer was.

"Oh, I got up late. I was getting ready to go in now." I followed him in the room. I ran my hand down the scratches on his back. He winced a little but didn't react. I sat down on the bed, stripped out of my clothes and jumped in the shower.

"James, before you go, I wanted to talk to you about something." I yelled out from the bathroom.

"I'm still here." I got a towel and walked in the room. I poured some of his favorite lotion in my hand and rubbed it on my skin. I put on one of the pieces of lingerie he loved and couldn't keep his hands off me when I wore it. I saw him staring at me licking his lips but his dick was still soft. I know he was trying hard to make me believe he was turned on.

"What did you wanna talk about?" He asked kissing on my neck. He was turning me on but he still had no arousal.

"Where were you today?" He stopped and froze. I picked up my glass, leaned on the dresser and waited for him to answer. I walked down the steps to pour myself something else to drink. I needed something to calm me down.

"I told you. I didn't leave the house. I was getting ready to go. What's this all about?" He said walking in the kitchen.

"And you're sure there's no other woman in your life?"

"Ci Ci, I told you already there's no one else." Men were so fucking stupid. If a woman ask you something more than once, most likely she already had the answer and proof and just waiting for him to say it.

I was looking in my phone to pull up the messages.

"Are you listening? Put your phone down."

"Funny thing about cell phones James is they have cameras and video on them." I looked at his face, which showed a sign of fear. Not like he was scared of me but him being caught.

"What are you talking about?"

"Ok, so you're going to continue with the lies?" He didn't say anything.

"Is this you James? Or wait maybe its Cream?" I shoved my phone in his face and watched him look at the photos.

"The best part is the video. Oh, you have to watch it." I took one last sip of my drink. My hands were shaking as he watched the video.

"You made love to her mouth right in the parking lot like you didn't have a wife at home." He went to speak and I put my hand up.

"Don't say shit to me you fucking bastard." I threw the glass and it caught him on the side of his head. I ran upstairs and locked the room door.

"Open the door Ci Ci."

"It's over James or should I call you Cream. James would've never cheated on me but Cream, that's the street nigga in you. Now him I can see it. So who were you when you were fucking her?" I started putting clothe son to leave.

"Ci Ci its not what it seems." I opened the door now that I was fully dressed.

"Is she the reason my husband can't make love to me anymore? The late-night phone calls; you coming home later every night. Is she?" He put his head down.

"Did you make love to her?"

"Why does that matter? I'm caught you know I cheated."

"Did you make love to her?"

"Ci Ci don't make me answer that."

"You not answering it gave me my answer. And you want to know why I asked that? I asked because if you did, it means you caught feelings for her and that it's more than what you're saying it is."

"Please don't leave."

"You got me fucked up if you think I'm staying here. James what did I do wrong?" I wiped my eyes as I stood at the front door with my keys.

65

"Nothing Ci Ci. Men don't always cheat because they want to. Sometimes they're put in situations they can't get out of." I laughed and wiped my nose with the back of my hand.

"Do you think I'm stupid? Everyone has a choice. You may not agree with the outcome of it but we always have a choice." He tried to touch me and I pushed him away.

"You had two to three seconds to change your mind before the first time you slept with her and you didn't. Then you continued. You know, I could have considered the first time was a mistake, but the rest weren't." His phone started buzzing but he wouldn't look at it.

"Answer it James. I'm sure its her calling to give you a new place to meet up at." He looked down at the phone and answered it. I could hear her voice on the other end telling him how she enjoyed it. The idiot had the volume up. He told her he would call her back.

"You fell in love with her didn't you."

"Ci Ci I'm…"

"Don't you dare say it?" I shook my head. He tried to hug me again and I pushed him off me. I walked out the door and went to my car. He came running behind me.

"I'll pick my son up from my sisters."

"I never meant to hurt you."

"No but you didn't love me either."

"How could you say that?"

"If you truly loved me, nothing that detective bitch said to you would've made you cheat on me."

"How do you know who she is?"

"I know that bitch from anywhere. She tried to get me to rat you out the first time I was arrested. She wanted you back then and now you can tell her she can have you."

"Ci Ci."

"What Cream?"

"Don't call me that?"

"Why not? That's what everyone else calls you. And since this marriage is over, I may as well follow suit."

"WHAT?" Was he really mad? The fucking nerve.

"You heard me. This marriage is over."

"No its not."

"Cream you just sat here and told me you made love to this woman, fell in love with her and when she called, I heard the entire conversation. There's no need to keep a man who don't want to be kept. Let's just get it over with so we can both move on with our lives."

"I didn't say any of that because you didn't let me answer." He's right I didn't but he didn't answer either.

"You stay with your detective and I'll find someone else."

"Ci Ci." He yelled out trying to chase my car.

"FUCK YOU NIGGA." I flipped him the bird. I drove a little down the street and parked my car on the side of the road. I broke down crying. I had snot and tears mixing together.

"Get out the car Ci Ci." He pulled my door opened and I snatched it back.

"Leave me the fuck alone Cream."

"You can't drive like this."

"I'm fine. Don't worry about me."

"What do you mean don't worry about you. You're my wife." I scoffed up a laugh. Now he wants to claim me after all the fucking he's been doing.

"Soon to be ex. Just go Cream." He leaned on the side of my car.

"I fucked up Ci Ci."

"You did exactly what you wanted to do."

"You think I wanted to cheat on you?"

"It doesn't really matter now." I grabbed tissue out the glove compartment.

"Go be with your side chick."

"Ci Ci don't do that."

"Don't do what? Acknowledge you're involved with another woman. What do you want me to do? Sit around praying you'll come to your senses and leave her to make our marriage work. I can't. Our time has come to an end. I mean I can't even get your dick to rise for me anymore." I said in a sarcastic tone.

"Can you answer me one more question?" I looked up at him with tears still racing down my face,

"What?"

"Did you use protection?" It took him a few seconds to answer.

"No."

"WHAT THE FUCK!!! I'm done with you. I banged my fist on the steering wheel.

"Calm down Ci Ci."

"You want me to calm down and you out here fucking bitches raw. What if she has something? Oh my God, what if she gets pregnant? You just gave zero fucks about me."

"Ci Ci, I wasn't thinking. No one is having babies by me but you."

"Wrong answer."

"What you mean wrong answer?"

"I will not have a baby by a man I'm not married to. Yes, my son is already here but you and I were together at the time."

"Don't do this Ci Ci." I saw his eyes becoming watery and I wanted to feel bad, but I couldn't. He broke my heart in a million pieces.

"You had me thinking I was crazy when your dick wouldn't rise and the while time its because you were fucking someone else. How could you do that me James? I was your wife. The woman you vowed never to cheat on or hurt." The longer I stayed there, it felt like someone was stabbing me in the chest.

"Goodbye Cream." I pulled off leaving him standing there.

I picked my son up and headed to the house I never wanted to return to. Everything was the same. I fed my son, bathed him and put him to bed. Cream called my phone over and over until I turned it off. I cried all night; a few times I vomited because I couldn't stop myself. This break up was killing me and only time would get me through it.

The next day I got my son and me up and went to a furniture store to order all new stuff. If I was staying back at home, I was decorating it the way I wanted; out with the old; in with the new.

****

71

I was driving to the club to drop the baby off to his bastard ass father. He claimed he was missing him in one of the text messages. I wasn't going to be petty.

I walked in and Damien took him from me but walked behind me up the steps. I could hear arguing coming from Cream's office.

"You in here on some blackmailing shit that caused me to lose my wife, my family and any future I had with her."

"Don't blame losing your family on me, you could've easily said no." I thought about barging in but what for?

"I could've said no and you would've sent my wife to jail." Damien looked at me and I shrugged my shoulders.

"Yea, she definitely would've gone to jail. Listen, there's no need to argue about it. Now we don't have to sleep around in hotels. I can come to your house or you can come to mine."

"Bitch is you crazy. I'm going to get my wife back and there's no way in hell I would allow you to step foot in a house she and I share."

"You mean shared." Damien shook his head.

72

"You can go now." He told her.

"Oh you're not coming home with me?"

"Are you serious right now? Get the fuck out of my office."

"You can stop talking to me like shit. I didn't ruin your marriage, you did." I had heard enough. I handed my son to Damien with his stuff and walked out.

I sat in my car and broke down again. He slept with her to keep me out of jail. I don't know why I would be arrested but that still doesn't change the fact he still had a choice. My phone rang and it was him.

"You couldn't bring him in yourself?"

"I brought him in but you were in a meeting and I didn't want to interrupt." I tried wiping my face but the tears wouldn't stop falling.

"Yea ok. Next time open the door and come in."

"No. I don't think it's a good idea. I'm not your wife anymore; I took those privileges away from myself. I will respect your establishment as if I were a guest."

"Then don't sit in front of my establishment crying." I was so pissed I hadn't moved from in front of the place and caught me.

"Goodbye Cream."

Cream

I didn't know who sent my wife those pictures but frankly I was happy this affair was out. I was tired of hiding and my dick was tired of fucking two women anyway.

When Damien brought my son in, I turned on my security cameras and saw my wife breaking down again in front of the club. I saw how bad I broke her and felt like shit.

I had her bring him here because I wanted to see her. She hasn't been answering her phone and I desperately wanted to be around her even if it were for a minute.

I didn't know the detective would show up at the same time she was bringing my son.

I turned everything off in my office, grabbed my son by the hand and locked up.

"I'll be back later or tomorrow. Damien you know what to do. Darius or Louis will be in but hit my cell if you need anything."

"Mmm hmm." I heard him say under his breath. He was team Ci Ci all day and I know he heard the bitch and me earlier.

I was putting my son in the car when Damien came out behind me.

"Listen boss. I don't like to get in your business, but you know that's my girl."

"What do you want?" I closed the back door.

"Was it worth it? I mean, I saw how much you loved her and you know she worshipped the ground you walk on. How could you do her like that?"

"You know what Damien. No, it wasn't worth it and I did what I had to do to keep her safe. You can call me what you want but I did it for her. Was it the right choice? No and at the time, I wasn't thinking about anything but keeping her out of jail." He gasped and put his hand over his chest.

"Jail?" I didn't elaborate any further. I got in my car and pulled off. I took my son to the park and then we stopped by my brothers' house who told me the shit that happened between him, Iesha and Monster.

"Damn I guess when it rains it pours." We let the kids play until they tired themselves out. I thought Ci Ci would call me but I guess she figured he was with his father, there was no need. I left her a message telling her I was home if she wanted to come get him, she could.

Ci Ci: *Can you keep him for the next few days?*

Me: *That's fine. Are you ok?*

Ci Ci I'm *ok. I just need some time to myself that's all.*

****

Four months went by and she and I were sharing custody and the drop-off was always at her sisters or my brothers. This last time she dropped him off, I hadn't heard from her in two days and I had Jr. so I called her. She answered on the third ring sounding like she was out of breath. I instantly got mad thinking she was fucking.

"I was just getting ready to call you. Can you drop him off? I'm at my mom's house." She said. I agreed and rushed over there to make sure I didn't catch a nigga leaving. I hated coming to this house. She opened the door in some spandex capris, a sports bra, sneakers and her hair was up in a ponytail.

She had the entire house changed from the paint, down to the furniture and rugs.

"It looks nice in here."

"Thanks. Iesha and I are the owners of this house and since she has her own, I'm taking over. Its already paid for so I only have to pay the taxes which she and I been doing."

"You look good Ci Ci."

"Thanks. I'm taking it one day at a time."

"Can you sit in here with him while I take a quick shower?"

"Go ahead, is it ok if I look around?"

"Sure, Jr can show you the place." My son was going on three and talking like a grown man. He showed me every room and stopped at his moms."

"This is you and mommy's room daddy." I grinned at him. He ran to his room to get me some toy he wanted to show me. She really did a nice job decorating.

I didn't wanna go by the bathroom and invade her privacy but there were mirrors all over the room and one showed her getting out the shower. She must've been working out for a while. She had abs forming in her stomach; I could see the muscles on her arms and legs as well. Her body was nice and had me adjusting myself.

I had been blowing off the detective since I lost my family. She didn't care as long as I wasn't with my wife she could care less. It was like she was jealous, and I didn't know why. Ci Ci never did anything to her.

"Come on daddy." My son took me out my thoughts and grabbed me by the arm to show me his toy and his room. I went downstairs when I heard the doorbell ring. It was the pizza guy dropping off food.

"Can we talk?" I asked after Jr went to sit in the living room to watch TV.

"Sure, what's up?" She put a slice of pizza on her plate.

"Ci Ci, I miss you like crazy. I know I fucked up but I wanna work on getting my wife and family back." She stared at me; then took a napkin and wiped her mouth. She sipped her drink and walked towards me to sit closer.

"How can you want to get your family back when your wife can't even get you aroused anymore?" I couldn't respond because at the time she was right.

"Do you know how it makes a woman feel knowing she can't please her husband because he's out there pleasing someone else?"

"Ci Ci it wasn't like that. I was juggling two women and my dick was tired."

"Did it work for her?" I put my head down.

"So your dick was tired for me but not her?"

"I'm not going to lie; I did catch feelings for her but not because I wanted to. She had me meeting her almost every day."

"Everyday? Damn."

"I wasn't doing anything but fucking her in the room. I would leave right after but I was used to seeing her face."

"You saw me everyday."

"Yes but I had a chance to miss you because we were both working. I saw her before work, sometimes after and then she stayed texting me all day."

"Sounds like a relationship to me." She said taking another bite.

"I can't really explain it but I don't love her."

"You don't love me."

"I do love you. In your heart you know that."

"I thought, I knew you loved me. You had me fooled though." She laughed to keep from crying.

"I fucked up Ci, but I know you still love me too." She took her forefingers to catch the tears that were trying to fall. I pulled here in between my legs.

"I know I hurt you real bad and there's nothing I can do to erase the pain except apologize."

"Cream, I don't think this is a good idea." She said as I kissed her neck. I put her hand on my dick to feel how hard I was. She pulled back and smiled.

"How did that happen?"

"You know what you do to me. Don't act like that."

She rolled her eyes.

"Ci Ci please. I want you back." She was about to have a nigga crying. I missed the shit outta her.

"I don't know Cream."

"Don't call me that."

"Why not, everyone else does."

"You're not everyone else. You're my wife; my other half." I could tell she was struggling with tryna make a decision.

"What do you want me to do? What can I do to prove, I want you and my family?" I kissed her lips and she invited my tongue in her mouth. We allowed them to fight for a few minutes.

"I love you Ci Ci."

"Cream I'm pregnant." I kissed her again.

"I know I have to get my family back now. Why are you working out like that?"

"I'm only a few weeks. The doctor said it's fine until I'm three months. I only walk the treadmill."

"It looked like you were getting abs."

"No fool. I suck my stomach in when I look in the mirror too see what I look like with them. I have been lifted those three-pound barbells on my arms and wearing weights on my ankles."

"What are you gonna do?"

"I'm going to keep the baby. I don't think I could get rid of it after I lost the first one."

"Are you sure?"

"Yea. What you don't want me to have it?" I wasn't sure where her head was because she always said she didn't want a baby outta wedlock and we're going through a lot right now.

"Yes. I hope it's a girl this time." I pulled her in front of me and rubbed her stomach. My phone rang and it was the detective bitch. This bitch stay calling at the wrong time.

"It's ok. I know you mess with her." I saw the hurt in her face.

"What did I tell you about calling me?" I barked the second I answered. She was yelling and Ci Ci dropped her pizza on the floor when she said it.

"WHAT???" I had to make sure I heard her correctly. When she repeated, she was pregnant, Ci Ci ran up the stairs crying. I hung the phone up on her and followed behind her. She was on the bed balled up in a fetal position.

"I'm sorry."

"Goodbye Cream." She said throwing the covers over her body.

"Ci Ci don't do this. We were just doing fine."

"That was before I heard your mistress say she was pregnant. I can't deal right now. Please just go." I put Jr. to bed, locked the doors and got in bed with her. I laid behind her on top of the covers and listened to her cry herself to sleep.

I knew that bitch wasn't pregnant because I saw her birth control pills in her drawer. They were popped out faithfully. I know sometimes it happens, but I also know that bitch probably found out I was here and did it on purpose. I was going to her house first thing tomorrow with a bunch of tests.

Ci Ci turned over to me in her sleep and snuggled under my arm. I moved her for a second to take my clothes off, got under the covers with her and let her sleep back on my chest. I know she missed me as much as I missed her. We just had to get over this roadblock to get back on track. I refused to lose my wife to this bitch. I was calling my cousin first thing in the morning; otherwise I had to take my chances and get rid of her myself.

Monster

Faith called after me an that fuck nigga got into a fight to tell me she was sitting at Newark airport. This bitch has never been to the states without her ex. I knew she had no idea what to do next and I should've left her dumb ass there.

I gave her the address to the hotel I was at and told her to take a cab because she had no idea what an Uber was.

I got out the shower to get ready for the club, opened the door for her an this horny bitch jumped on me right away. I know I just fucked my ex but I'm a man and as long as my dick got hard, I was game. I made sure to send her down to the store next door to grab some condoms. I just got a clean bill of health an there was no way I was risking it on her ass.

"Miguel is coming here to take that bitch back with him, so we have to get the shit over an done with."

"Do you have the truck rented and you're sure about the hotel he's staying at?"

"Yes. I heard him reserving it. He had his office door open and didn't know I was listening."

"What's your beef with this chick anyway? I mean you going hard to get rid of her?"

"Miguel is my man. He has been from the first time we got together and this bitch thinks she can just come here an snatch him away. I don't think so." I had to laugh at her because her accent was strong as hell and it seemed like she we speaking Spanish by how fast she was going.

"Maybe he sprung on that pussy." She threw her brush at my head.

"Fuck that bitch and her dirty ass pussy." I laughed at her dumb ass. She was stuck on this nigga that didn't want her.

"Let's go then. I'll drop you off to the truck an you have to do the rest." I told her grabbing my keys.

"Don't worry about any of that."

I dropped her off and headed to dinner and then the club with this Violet woman. She was gorgeous and I could see why this nigga wasn't leaving her.

She and I danced a few songs before I dipped off to VIP. I saw this nigga stand behind her with two big ass dudes. I saw the bitches lusting after him like he was a celebrity or

87

some shit.

I watched him feel all over her on the dance floor then carry her ass out. I sent the text to Faith to let her know it was now or never. I hopped in my car and parked a few spots down from where she parked the truck. She text me they walked in before she got there but that she was going to wait. I ain't have shit to do so I sat back in my car smoking and texting Iesha.

Me: *Missing you and that pussy.*

Iesha: *Monster what we did was wrong. I lost my man over it.*

Me: *Who cares. You got me back now.*

Iesha: *Monster I love him, and I hurt him bad. I will always love you but he has my heart now.*

Me: *Fuck that meet me tomorrow.*

Iesha: *No.*

Me: *You better or I'm killing him.*

Iesha: *Where?*

I told her to meet me somewhere else because this bitch wanted to stay the night and stay an extra day. She agreed.

I looked up and saw the chick V running out and dude

was behind her. She look like she was crying and that's when Faith stepped on the gas and sped up. Her dumb ass crashed into the back of a parked car, that hit the cab. Violet never saw the shit coming as I watched her body fly in the air. That nigga lost it.

I saw Faith speed off and I pulled off a few minutes later. Cops an ambulance got there in no time closing off the scene. I met her ass at the truck drop off and went back to the hotel. She was nervous as hell and getting on my nerves at the same time.

"Do you think she's dead?"

"I don't know. Your ass should've stayed around to see."

"Don't be a smart ass."

"I thought you had this. What happened to all that shit you were talking?"

"I got her didn't I?"

"Yea but you hit a parked car first so I'm sure the impact would've really killed her if you got to her instead."

"Oh well, if she ain't dead I'll get her ass. Reggie and

some guys are waiting at her house. They are going to light her ass up when she walks in."

"Damn you gangsta as hell over that man."

"What can I say? He got me dick dizzy."

"Yea; but that chick must have him pussy dizzy because it doesn't look like he's leaving her alone anytime soon."

"Whatever. Just give me some of that dick so I can go to sleep." She was crazy as hell but her head game was on point.

Iesha

I can't believe I let that nigga Monster get in my head the way he did. I loved Darius with all my heart and after I fucked my ex back at the room, I know that more than ever.

I never planned on seeing him again but now he's claiming he'll kill Darius if I don't come see him. I was stuck between a rock and a hard place, but I put myself there. I was going to meet him but just to let him know nothing was coming of us and if he didn't like it, I would have to take matters into my own hands.

I know Darius would do anything to protect me and its only fair I do the same thing for him.

I sent my sister a message to tell her where I was meeting his dumb ass. I wasn't trying to impress him so I put on jeans, a t-shirt and a pair of Uggz. I pulled up at the spot he told me to meet him at.

"What's up sexy?" He pulled the chair out for me.

"I'm here. What do you want?" I asked him rolling my eyes.

"Iesha, I came back for you. Why are you acing like you don't care about a nigga anymore?"

"Monster, I will always care and even have a small place in my heart for you but what we had is over. If you would've come back for me sooner, I probably would've left with you but my heart belongs to Darius."

"Oh your heart belongs to this nigga?" He showed me a photo of him and Sky at the mall with her daughter. It was funny because Sky asked me what color Jordan's I wanted her to get for Summer that same day.

I knew all about the outing but I let him believe he had the upper hand. Sky was terrified of me so I knew she didn't even think twice about fucking with Darius.

"You think I care if he's out with someone else when he caught me with you? I got his heart so I'm not worried."

"Well you have mine too. You're just going to throw away what we had?"

"Monster you threw it away when you got caught. I'm sorry about how things between us ended but you have to let me go."

"Fuck that Iesha." I stood up to leave. I knew his temper and sometimes it caused him to have a hand problem. I refuse to allow that to happen with a man I'm not even with.

"It's over Monster. Go back to Phila and find a new chick." He grabbed my arm and I felt someone tug me from behind.

"I see you can't leave this nigga alone." Darius said shaking his head.

"It's not like that Darius."

"I don't care what it's like. This is twice I caught you with the same fuck boy." Monster stood up and they were about to go at it. I tried to push Darius out the door and he snatched away from me.

"Fine. If y'all want to fight, then go ahead; I'm over both of you acting like kids." I stepped outside and went to my car. These niggas were not about to have me in an early grave over who is the bigger man.

I drove to the movies to clear my head. Monster was sending me all these death threat messages about Darius, and Darius was calling my phone back to back. I just shut the shit off. I sat in the theatre watching the movie Creed and started crying for no reason.

My head was hurting as so was my heart. I screwed over a good man for a no good man. I needed my dad, my sister or somebody to tell me everything would be ok but no one seemed to be available.

After the movie, I shut my phone back on and had missed messages from those two fools. I didn't even bother opening them. I put my phone on the counter when I got home.

I walked in the kitchen and smelled the food. The nanny made some spaghetti with garlic bread and a salad. She and I sat there talking while Summer babbled in the high chair. I missed Darius mom since she went to Puerto Rico to visit her sister and her kids. She had been over there a month already, but it feels like forever.

I gave Summer her bath and put her to bed. She was a little fussy because she was teething.

I laid in the bed watching TV when my bedroom door busted open with Darius. I was over his shit and if he came here to argue about my ex, I wasn't going to entertain his ass.

He could go back home with that.

Darius

I saw Iesha's car parked at home and all the lights were out except the TV in her room. I was pissed when I saw her ass at the restaurant she told Ci Ci she would be at. I was still in love with her and I would never allow anyone to hurt her; together or not.

I went in, locked her door and was on my way upstairs when I saw her cell phone on the counter. No wonder she didn't read shit I sent. I saw the shit was unlocked as always. I told her plenty of times to put a lock on her phone but at this moment I was glad she didn't.

I saw messages from me and that other dude. I saw him texting her and she told him I had her heart and didn't wanna have anything else to do with her. I felt fucked up when I read the message saying if she didn't show up he would kill her. She only went to keep me safe. I guess he wasn't happy about the conversation they had because he really went in on the threats against me and her. I was shocked that he came back for her only to try and kill her for not wanting him. I put the phone back and went upstairs.

"What Darius? If you here on some bullshit you can go. I'm over both of you." She sucked her teeth and rolled on her side. I kneeled down in front of her and kissed her.

"What are you doing?" She asked jumping up.

"Iesha, I get it. You needed to get him out your system. You went about it the wrong way but I get it."

"You don't have to make excuses for me. I should've never hurt you like that." She started crying and stood up.

"It's not an excuse for you. I'm not dumb either. I don't think you went there intentionally to sleep with him but you definitely could've stopped it."

"I know and you're right. I never meant to hurt you and I still love you but I also know you won't get past this. I still want us to be friends for Summer."

"Shut up Iesha and come here." I yanked her closer to me and kissed her aggressively. I lifted her pajamas over her head and laid her down on the bed. I kissed all over her body, in between her thighs and submerged myself in her wetness. She came instantly and didn't stop until I let up.

I came out of all my clothes and tried to get on top but she pushed me off her and got on top. She made her way to my manhood and took him in whole.

"Fuck baby." I couldn't hold it in and came in her mouth. I sat on my elbows and watched her suck the life out of me.

"Was that good for you?" She asked coming up to kiss me. I felt myself becoming hard again. She slid down and cried as she was riding me.

"Baby, what's wrong?" I moved her hands from her eyes.

"I'm so sorry Darius. I can't believe I fucked up like this. I love you so much."

"I'm not going anywhere." I changed positions and got on top of her. I made love to her erasing any doubt she had about us.

"I love you Iesha."

"I love you too. Are you going to be with someone else?"

"No baby. I don't want anyone but you. That's why I'm

here. I couldn't be without you." She smiled and wiped her eyes. We kissed and finished sexing most of the night.

"Darius, I have to tell you something." She looked up at me as she laid on my chest.

"What?"

"Jeremy is going to come after both of us."

"I know. I'm not worried about that. All I'm worried about is my baby in your stomach."

"Huh? What baby?"

"I guess you didn't find out yet. Your pussy feels the same way it did when you were pregnant with Summer and you were running from me when I hit it from the back. You love that position and always throw it back at me."

"Shit."

"What do you mean shit?"

"I'm mad you knew before me." She laughed.

"I know my pussy."

"And yours it is baby."

"Iesha don't do that again." I moved the hair out her face.

"I swear I won't ever hurt you like that again."

"You ready for my son?" She shook her head yes.

"Can I ask you a question Darius?"

"Did you sleep with Sky when you found out?"

"No. That wasn't even a thought. Plus, you got that woman scared to even sit by me."

"Good, that's how I want it."

We got up the next day and I ran to the store to get tests to prove what I already knew. She indeed was having another one of my kids. I think it was about time to give her my last name. She made an appointment for Monday and I was going with her. She also told them she wanted both of us to get tested because she slipped up and fucked dude without a condom. I couldn't do shit but respect it.

"I'm sorry baby."

"It's fine. I respect the fact that you not only told me but signed us both up to get tested. I love you for that."

Monday came quick and we were both excited to find out how far along she was. In my mind I was praying it was my baby. She fucked dude two weeks ago and I would be pissed if it were his.

The nurses took out blood for the STD test and walked out. We had the results sent to the house; there was no need to make an appointment to come here for that. The doctor came in, said hello, sat down and squirted the gel on her stomach and turned he machine towards us.

"Wow, this is a very active baby already." She said smiling at both of us. She moved the thing around and her smile turned upside down.

"What's up doc?" I asked her looking at her facial expression. Iesha squeezed my hand as we waited for her to answer.

"Well you are three and half months and I hope you're ready for two more people to join your family." The look of shock hit both of our faces.

"Twins. How the hell did that happen? And why didn't I know I was pregnant?" Iesha asked sounding like she was pissed.

"Well this happens a lot in women where they still get their periods, and some have no symptoms at all. I am a little worried because your body is underweight to be carrying two babies. I'm going to need you to eat more and I'm sending you home with prenatal vitamins. I want to see you gained at least ten or more pounds by the next appointment." She had Iesha clean herself off and handed her the prescription for the vitamins. I helped her off the table and kissed her stomach.

"Damn, I got that lethal sperm for real." She hit me softly in the arm. We walked out hand in hand out of the doctors' office.

I closed passenger side door and felt a pain in my side. I found myself hunched over on Iesha's lap trying to breathe.

"Darius are you ok?" She asked sounding like she was crying but I couldn't answer.

"Yes, my boyfriend was shot please help him." I heard her screaming in the phone to 911.

"Darius, the ambulance is on the way. Stay with me baby."

"Sir, can you hear me. Try and stay awake. Remember you have two babies coming into the world that need you." The doctor said to me as I went in and out of consciousness.

Cream

I left Ci Ci this morning, ran home to get dressed then took my ass to CVS to pick up some damn pregnancy test. I called that stupid bitch to tell her I was coming over. I bet she won't be expected my ass to make her take a piss test. I was obsessed with getting my family back and she damn sure wasn't going to stand in my way.

I stood in that line with six of them in my hand. I don't know why I had that many because after the first one I knew would say negative, I was good. I got my STD and AIDS test back and everything was good. I don't know what I was thinking sleeping with her without a condom. I was really on some fuck shit plus I wouldn't dare sleep with my wife again until I got the results back.

I got to the detective house and as usual she was ready to fuck but I had other shit on my mind. I grabbed her hand and led her to the bathroom.

"Let's take these test."

"WHAT?" She yelled out crossing her arms. I knew

right then she wasn't.

"Piss on these tests right now?"

"Who the hell are you talking to? I don't have to do shit." I was over this bitch blackmailing me and playing games. I pulled my gun out and put it right on her temple.

"You better do it now or you won't be seeing shit but God; an that's if he allows you in heaven after all this shit you down here doing." She still stood there not moving like I was playing. I cocked that motherfucker back and the bitch ripped one of those boxes open real quick.

"Nah, you're going to open and piss on everyone. Whatever the results; I want to make sure they all say the same thing."

"How am I supposed to do that?"

"Easy; go then hold it; go on the next one; hold it an keep doing it until there's some on each one of them."

"I don't have to take one of these."

"Oh but you do. You see you ruined my marriage, then you called me up when I was trying to make it right with my wife telling me you're pregnant, which by the way she heard since you yelled it in the phone and you're going to give me that DVD before I leave here." She rolled her eyes and did what I said.

"Just like I thought your dumb ass ain't even pregnant. I saw your pills that you popped out faithfully. Pass me some tissue." I wrapped all six of them up and was taking them to my wife to prove she wasn't having my baby.

"Why are you doing this?" She asked as I pushed her into the office of her house. She went into some safe and took out three DVD's of what appeared to be copies.

"Nah, I want to see what else is in there." She took out paperwork that had Kelly's name on it. On top of the folder it said clear as day CASE CLOSED! This bitch was fucking with me the entire time. There were files on other people too but my cousin was underneath all of it.

"Why were you blackmailing me if her case was closed? Matter of fact, why are you looking for this man?" I asked pointing at Miguel.

"He's some big time kingpin that has ties over here and were about to set him up with a guy that was just released from jail." She said looking mad.

I took everything she had in the safe along with any USB's I saw and her fucking laptop. I wasn't playing any more games with this bitch.

"She won't love you like I could."

"That's the problem. She loved me too good and I took her for granted. I should've never allowed you to play me like that."

"You're telling me that you don't have any feelings for me and you can just walk away from what we had?"

"The feelings I thought I had for you were built on lies. Lies you told to blackmail me for some dick."

"That was the only way I could get you to pay me any attention."

"You're dam right it was. But you should know I would do anything to protect my wife and my family. It's sad you went through all that to fuck. It's many men out here you could've been with. Why would or should I say why did you choose me?"

"I've been infatuated with you since I came across your

file. When I saw you, it was like love at first sight and I had to have you." I shook my head thinking about what CiCi said. She was right about her wanting me from the beginning.

"Let me make this clear right here, right now. Don't come for me or anyone in my family again. The last thing you want is to be on my bad side."

"Then why didn't you just kill me?"

"I know the FEDS is watching me. Every move I make is being recorded. Do you think I'm stupid? But know this." I got closer to make sure she heard me.

"Don't think for one second you're untouchable and that I wasn't thinking about killing you myself. My reach is longer than you think and you have one time to fuck with my wife and you'll be touched before you can blink."

"What?"

"I see you all in your feelings over me and that's cool. But you better leave it all right here." I picked everything up and walked out. I wasn't worried about her coming behind me or telling. She knew I had her ass by the balls, and it was nothing she could do about it.

I went by Ci Ci's house happy as hell I had all the ammunition, I needed to get her back. She walked out the front door with my son crying. I left everything in the car and ran up to her.

"What's wrong? Are you hurt? Is the baby ok? Is my son alright?" I fired off question after question then checking my son.

"Where have you been? Everyone has been trying to reach you for the last hour."

"Oh shit. I left my phone at the house."

"Your mom is on her way back from Puerto Rico with your cousin."

"Why, what happened?" She looked at me like she was about to give me the worst news ever.

"Baby. Darius was shot and he hasn't woke up yet." I felt like the wind was knocked out of me. I felt the tears leaving my eyes unexpectedly as I tried to get to my car.

"James you can't drive like that. Give me the keys." I didn't want to because I knew she was going to take forever to get to the hospital, but she was right, we'd probably get in an accident on the way there.

To my surprise she got us there faster than I expected. We walked in and Iesha was on the phone and passed it to me.

"Hello."

"Just know it's going to get handled. Iesha told me who it was and I'm already on it." I heard Miguel's voice say over the phone before he disconnected the call. He never spoke much on his phone in case the Feds were listening.

"What happened?"

"He was helping me get in the car when I saw his eyes grow big and he fell over on my lap. I tried to lift him and I saw blood coming out his side. I looked over and saw Monster smiling in his truck. I grabbed the gun from under the seat, cocked that shit and walked over to him with it pointed at him. I let off several shots but he pulled off."

Iesha told me what happened as we waited for the doctors to come out. When they finally did, they told us Darius was shot in the back; inches from his spine as well as his shoulder. He lost a lot of blood and had to get a blood transfusion. They put him in a medically induced coma because he kept seizing.

Iesha was a wreck but we all sat in my brothers' room for a few days waiting for him to wake up. It was up to him at this point. Sky came up and took Summer so Iesha could stay there, and Ci Ci had Jr staying with my mom when she left. I stood up and went by Darius bedside.

"Come on man, you have to wake yourself up. You're wasting too much time in here laid up trying to catch up on some sleep. You need to take your girl home and play with your daughters. They need you man; I need you and so does ma. You have to get up." I found myself breaking down. Ci Ci grabbed my hand and took me outside to get some air.

"Darius is going to wake up soon. You know he's too stubborn to stay asleep." Her voice calmed me down like it always did when I was upset over something.

"I can't watch him die."

"Baby he's not going to. He's just sleeping that's all. He'll be up soon."

"Thanks baby." I kissed her on the lips.

"Did you eat today?" I asked rubbing her stomach.

"I had a sandwich earlier when you were asleep in the room."

"Ci Ci you have to eat it's after 8. Come on let's go see what they have in the cafeteria." I took her hand and was happy to see they were still open.

The grill was going so I had them make her a well-done cheeseburger and French-fries. I got her some chips and a soda. She was feeding me a fry when the detective walked in with a smirk on her face. I know it was because she saw my wife.

"I'm about to smack the shit out of her." Ci Ci said making me laugh.

"Don't worry about her. She's jealous of you and what you have."

"Oh yea and what do I have?"

"Me. Always and forever."

"Hmmmm." She said and pecked my lips. We heard someone suck their teeth and it was her.

"Remember what the fuck I said when it comes to my wife. My reach is longer than you think." She rolled her eyes and walked out.

"What did you tell her?"

"I'll tell you about that later. Let's go back and check on my brother." We stayed in the hospital all night with him and Iesha.

I talked to my cousin a few times who said the nigga must've vanished because he was nowhere to be found but there was a $2,000,000 bounty out on his head. It was just a matter of time. Money talks bullshit walks.

Ci Ci

James and I left the hospital for the night after that bitch saw us in the cafeteria. I don't know what happened between them two, but it was obvious she was in her feelings over it.

He still wanted to tell me what happened when he saw her that morning. He asked could he stay the night and I was fine with that; I know he didn't want to be alone with his brother in the hospital.

We put Jr to bed and I went to get in the shower; I heard the curtain open and he was behind me. Surprisingly, he didn't try anything and washed both of our bodies. He did his normal routine which was dry me off and make sure I had my pajamas on before himself.

He went downstairs to get us something to drink and came back up with all sorts of shit. There was a brown bag with white sticks coming out of it, a laptop, files and some damn USB's that he placed on the dresser. He sat in front of me and grabbed my hands.

"Baby, I can't imagine what you went through when you found out I was cheating. I know I broke your heart and that was never my intention. She taped you and the girls kill Kelly and the only way stopping her from showing the DA, was if I slept with her.

You were right, it was a choice and I should've thought about it before I dove right in without looking. It was a one-time thing but she continued harassing me, so I gave her what she wanted. You asked me if I made love to her and I can honestly say I was close to it, but I didn't. She wasn't you and I couldn't see me giving my all to her. You asked if I loved her and my answer is no. I would never love a woman the way I love you. I think I couldn't get hard for you that night because I knew I was wrong and couldn't even force myself to sleep with you knowing what I was doing. She had me acting out of character and I took it out on you." I had tears coming down my eyes.

"I love you so much Ci Ci and I am truly sorry for hurting you like that and even going as far as disrespecting you. I promised you at the very beginning I would never hurt you

114

and I did. I promise to make it up to you for the rest of my life if you allow me. Will you please be my wife again?" He said with glassy eyes.

"I love you too James and I'm sorry you were pushed in a corner like that to protect me. It just proves that you will go above and beyond to protect your family and I respect that. I hate that it came down to you sleeping with her and almost ruining our marriage. I feel like someone ripped my heart out when I found out and it killed me; then I heard you outside the office and felt like shit because it was all for me. Baby, I'm sorry too. I should've let you explain what really happened." He pulled me down on top of him on the bed.

"Oh don't get it twisted, there were other ways you could've went about it instead of giving her something that belonged to me. I wish you would've talked to me about it and maybe we could've did something else."

"You know I could've killed her but because we're still on the FEDS radar. I didn't want to take any chances and I didn't have the video footage."

"Did you enjoy it?"

"I don't want to discuss that with you. Just know she was an annoying fuck." He said making both of us laugh. I guess I could live with that answer because I wasn't sure I wanted to know anyway.

"Did you miss me James?" I asked in between him kissing on my neck.

"You know I did. I missed everything about you. How you wake up in the morning, go to sleep, brush your teeth, your hair, cook."

"Ok baby, I get it." He touched my pearl with his tongue and inserted two fingers at the same time.

"Oh God baby." My body shook and I came all over him.

"Is this still mine?" He asked while he was sucking.

"Yes, hell yes." I gripped the hell out of the sheets, arched my back and gave him the biggest orgasm I think my body ever had. I was breathing so hard he came up to make sure I was good.

"Go for a ride baby." I climbed on top and drifted slowly down his pole. It was like we both needed this because

116

we exploded soon after. I wanted to give him all of me, so I made my way down to my favorite place.

"Ci you don't have to."

"Are you still my husband?"

"You know I am. Ain't nobody ever taking this spot." He said holding on to the back of my head.

"Ok. Let me please my husband."

"Shitttttt do your thing baby." I took a sip of the ice-cold water he brought me and put my mouth back around him. He jumped back moaning. I licked under his balls and played with them at the same time. My tongue slid up and went in and out the tip driving him crazy. I made him sit up on his elbows and watch me.

"Yo, I really have the best wife in the world. Do that shit Ci." He was egging me on. I went faster and wet his dick up so much he couldn't take it. His legs were shaking as I jerked and sucked until his cum came out erupting like a volcano.

"Ahhhhhh suck it all baby. Yea just like that. Aww shit girl."

"Mmmmm give me all of it." I told him. He grabbed me up when I was done and turned me over.

His tongue went in and out my ass, back and forth to my pussy. My man had me literally screaming and climbing the headboard to get to the walls. Whoever said make-up sex was just ok, was telling a dam lie.

"Oh God baby. Please make me cum one more time. It's right there." He was playing in my pussy. My pearl was hard but every time I was ready to explode, he would stop.

"Tell me what I want to hear."

"James Thomas it's all yours baby. I swear I won't ever give your pussy away."

"Yea, that's what I wanna hear."

"Oh God, Oh God James I'm cumming, oh God, here I cummmmm." His face was covered in my juices. I fell back on the bed out of breath.

"I love you Cecilia Renee Thomas."

"I love you too baby. Oh my God, I missed you so much." I found myself crying again.

"I'm not ever fucking up again." He told me as he

wiped my tears.

"Shit, Ci Ci you're pussy definitely has me strung." I grinned when he said that. His mom used to tell him he was strung on me a while ago.

"You have me dick dizzy, so I guess we're in the same boat." He laughed and pulled me closer to him. I heard his phone ringing in the middle of the night, but he was knocked out.

"Hello." Yup, I answered it.

"Hey sis. I just called to let you guys know Darius is up and he wants to talk to his brother."

"Tell him I said forget him then."

"Baby." He didn't move.

"Baby. Wake up." I nudged him.

"Hold on Iesha. I put that ass to sleep."

"I know that's right." She said laughing.

"James baby."

"Yea, what's wrong?" He popped up.

"Darius is awake and he wants to talk to you." He kissed my lips then took the phone and started talking. I could

119

see him getting a little emotional while they spoke. I wanted to give him their privacy, but he grabbed me by the arm and had me lay on his lap. After he hung up, he asked me to come up there with him later.

It was a little after six so I got up and ran to the store to get breakfast food to cook. I was supposed to go shopping a few days ago but with what happened to Darius I didn't.

I saw a blue detective car put their lights on and stop behind me.

****

"Where did you go? I wanted to taste you this morning." James asked when I answered the phone.

"She is really going to make me fuck her up James." I saw detective Williams getting out the car.

"Who? Where are you?" I heard him panicking through the phone.

"I'm coming back from the store and this bitch pulled me over." I watched her walk to my car with a smirk on her face.

"I'll be right there." He yelled in the phone.

"Baby, Jr is in the house. You can't leave him." I had to remind him because he was about to rush out and forget.

"Well keep me on the phone."

"License and Registration." Detective Williams asked and kept her hand on her waist.

"Damn, don't I get a please?" I reached over to get what she asked for and when I went to give it to her, she punched me in the face.

"Oh no the fuck you didn't just punch me. Move bitch." I tried to open my car door and she held it closed with her leg.

"I wish you would get out this fucking car. I'll shoot your ass right here." I had James on the phone yelling. I knew he was pissed after hearing everything.

"I see you're in your feelings over my husband but guess what he's mine. And yes, he made love to me all night long so whatever thoughts you have about him you need to get them out your head. He may have slipped up but he will never leave me; you can bet your last dollar on that shit."

"Well I can tell you your husbands dick felt so good in my mouth and when he fucked me and had me screaming his

121

name there were no thoughts of you on his mind." She had a smug look on her face and it tore me up to hear she was having a good time with my husband.

I punched that bitch hard as hell in her stomach and pulled the fuck off. I was flying home and when I got there, James was outside with his mom and my son.

"She did that to your face?" He examined it.

"I'm fine baby."

"No you're not. I'm about to end this bitch." He went to step off the porch and five fucking cop cars pulled up in my driveway with her stupid ass.

"Put your hands on your head." They were standing behind their car doors with their guns pointing towards me. I refused to let that bitch see me upset. She walked over to me and snatched my arms to place them in handcuffs.

"I'll be right behind you." He kissed my lips.

"I told you not to come for my wife. You just fucked up." He said in her ear but I heard him. She looked scared as hell.

She pushed my head down and put me in her car. I

think she knew he would follow her if I weren't in the car. I smiled at her each time she glanced at me in the mirror.

"You think you're funny bitch." She snapped.

"No, I just know that you are about to see a side of my husband that I've never seen. I would hate to be you right now."

"Whatever. If he knows what's good for him, he better not lay a finger on me."

"And what's good for my husband besides my pussy since you seem to know him better than me?"

"I know that he loves my fat ass and the way my pussy squirts when he fucks me."

"Is that all you can go off. I mean you have to give me more to go on than that. Did my husband make love to you? Did he let you feel his tongue snake in and out your pussy and make you climb walls? Does he eat that ass you claim he loves? Can you make him say your name? No wait! I got it. Is he willing to leave me and give you his last name and everything he has?" I could see her getting pissed.

"Bitch your pussy ain't all that." I laughed so hard she

started driving erratic making me slide back and forth.

"You think my man would be acting like this if I had whack ass pussy? Oops that's how he acts with you because he can care less about you or your feelings." I stared at how pitiful she looked.

"You fucked around and fell in love with a married man thinking he was going to leave his wife. He knows you're a piece of shit by the way you came at him. Any woman that has to black mail a man to get some dick is pathetic. You knew he would never do it willingly, so you have to find another way to get it."

"Shut the fuck up bitch." She yelled pointing a gun in my face. The door swung open and I thought James was going to be arrested.

"Yo bitch, what the fuck are you doing? Get that gun out my wife's face." The other cops had to pull him back from her.

"James, baby I'm ok." He was flipping out.

"James, look at me." He stopped for a second and stared at me.

"I'm ok. Please calm down. Jr doesn't need both of his parents in jail. I love you." She snatched me away before I was able to kiss him.

I sat in the jail cell for all of ten minutes before the same lawyer Mr. Friedman came in with the captain, the detective and another lawyer.

"Mrs. Thomas are you ok?" I shook my head yes.

"Would you like to press charges on detective Williams?"

"Press charges?" She stood in the corner biting her nails.

"Yes, after the routine stop she did on you, it showed her attacking you in the car in which you defended yourself."

"I'm not sure what I want to do right now. I just need to get to a hospital to make sure my baby is ok."

"Your baby? You're pregnant." The captain and other lawyer looked back at the detective and my lawyer had the biggest grin on his face.

"Yes I am. I'm three months along. And you know the first trimester is always the most critical do you think my baby is ok?" I was laying it on them thick.

"Ms. Thomas on behalf of the entire department we would like to apologize for the actions of Ms. Williams. In no way, were we aware of the way she acted towards you."

"You need to check audio/ video inside the car as well. Ms. Williams was saying some pretty harsh things to me about my husband and then out of nowhere pulled a gun on me. If I'm not mistaken, that's against the law isn't it?"

"Yes ma'am. A gun should've never been taken out in that car especially when you were restrained by handcuffs. Again, we apologize for her actions."

"I don't blame you sir. I just want to get my baby checked out between the stress and erratic driving; I hope everything's ok." Mr. Friedman can you please take me to my husband?" He put his hand on my lower back to escort me out.

"Oh Captain, isn't this the same woman that arrested me previously on charges against my husband. Wait, aren't you also the one that had my husband arrested at his home for someone falsely accusing him of assault but you raided his house as well? I don't know but if you ask me, this is definitely

126

harassment at its best. Have a good day Captain and I hope you get this under control quickly." I said running to James.

He picked me up and kissed me. He rubbed on my stomach and we both looked up and everyone was staring. That was perfect because they knew I wasn't lying about being pregnant.

"Ms. Williams my office NOW!" She didn't move quickly enough because he screamed at her again.

"James you know I'm about to sue the shit out of this department and trust me when I say we'll all be rich as hell after this. Well, I will be because you already are but who cares; add a few more millions to your bank account." He shook our hands and left. I rode to the hospital with him. I did get checked out in the ER before we went up to see Darius.

Monster

I was on my way out of town when my sister called talking about how she needed to see me right away. I didn't know why things were always urgent with her and half the time it don't be shit.

I made a detour in the middle of the road; cars were blowing and shit. I flipped the finger to all of them. I got to her house and she opened the door looking like she was crying and scared at the same time.

"What's up sis? Why you over here acting like someone is trying to kill you?" I stepped inside.

"I fucked up." She cried.

I didn't know what she was talking about because the plan we had in place was working perfectly from what she told me.

I locked the door and followed her in the living room. Her hands were shaking as she tried to take a sip of her drink.

"Come on sis, you're making me nervous. What you mean you fucked up?"

"Well Cream found out I lied about the pregnancy; then he took all my files; including the one with all his cousins information. My laptop, USB's, the DVDs everything."

"So what. That just means we'll find something else to get him on."

"No, I fucked up worse than that."

I don't know what was worse than that. Unless she killed his wife or some shit. I waited for her to finish drinking again to speak.

"I pulled his wife over today."

"Ok. For what?"

"Just because; it was on some petty shit."

"So what happened?"

"Just looking at her pissed me off so I punched her in the face then she punched me in the stomach. I made a call to dispatch that an officer was assaulted, and the assailant was on the run. We went to the house and I had her arrested. But the worst part was when we were in the car, she was talking shit an I put the gun in her face."

"YOU DID WHAT?" I was yelling at her. How fucking

dumb could she be? Even I know that was stupid.

"The one thing I told you when we came up with the plan was not to fuck with his wife. What were you thinking?" She started crying harder.

"I know, I know but I was in my feelings because he chose her over me. Fuck that bitch, that's supposed to be my man."

"Are you listening to yourself? You're a fucking detective and you did some dumb shit and tried hiding behind the badge. I bet your ass got fired, didn't you?" She shook her head yes.

"You have to get out of here. That nigga is about to hunt your ass down like an animal looking for his prey. I'm surprised he's not here right now."

"What about you? You shot his brother you don't think they coming for you too?"

"Oh, I know they are. But you see, he's still laid up on the hospital and I'm on my way out of the country. They won't find my black ass back in these states anytime soon. Get your shit so we can get the fuck out of here."

I went to the bathroom and could still hear her crying. I thought I heard the door but she couldn't be that dumb to answer it if someone knocked.

I put my ear to the door and didn't hear shit. I stepped out and the house was on fire. I ran through looking for my sister and she was lying in a pool of her own blood. Shot in the middle of her forehead. *Fuck! I can't believe he killed her.*

Damn that nigga wasted no time coming for her. I was about to step outside when I heard shit falling from the ceiling. I guess it was debris; I went out the bathroom window and tried to run around the house when someone stopped me.

"Oh no nigga. You're not going anywhere."

"Who the hell are you?" I asked her. She grinned and told me not to worry about it. I got in the car with her and watched Cream get back in his car and pull off.

"We're about to get him, his brother and those bitches they're with." I looked over at this woman trying to figure out who she was and what beef she had with them. She let me off to my car.

"When it's time I'm going to call you. I expect you to

131

come running. If I have to come looking for you, I will lead them niggas straight to you."

"What?"

"See there's a $2,000,000 bounty on your head. It's nothing to collect and live off that. Now be a good boy and handle what you need to in P.R."

"How the hell you know where I'm going?"

"I've been watching you. I like the way you move. That's all you need to know. I'll be in touch." She said and pulled off. I got to the airport and hopped my flight to P.R. I told Faith where to meet me.

After we fucked, we discussed what our next move was. But I still couldn't get that woman out my head. It's like I know her from somewhere I just don't know where.

Iesha

Darius came home three weeks after being shot by my ex. He had to use a cane because he refused to sit in a wheelchair. The physical therapist came over five days a week to help him. He acted like such a baby when she left too. I swear I already had two kids instead of one.

He was staying in my house because it was a ranch style home with no stairs. His house had stairs leading everywhere in his house; including stepping up just to go in the kitchen; it really was ridiculous. He went by there a few times but came back.

I didn't mind though because he was back in my life right where I needed him to be. I was still dealing with the fact he was shot because of me and it was taking a toll on me. I blamed myself and no matter how much he said he didn't place any blame on me.

I drove him to his office because he was tired of sitting in the house. Amir and a new security guard helped him up the steps.

"Thank you guys. I appreciate you helping him." I told both of them. The guys had a pretty good team that worked in the bar, except for that snake Mike we no longer have to worry about.

"Come here baby." He called me over to him and sat me down on his lap facing him. I knew what he wanted because his dick was poking through his sweats. I locked the door and went back to him. I stripped naked and helped him; then placed him inside me.

"Shit, Iesha. You just don't know how much I've missed this." He said while I rode him.

"I missed it too. Are you ok though?"

"Fuck yea. Don't take it easy on me. I need you to fuck me like you normally do."

"You sure?" He lifted me up and made me fuck him harder. He couldn't thrust into me the way he wanted to, and this was the way he wanted it and that's what he got.

"Darius, I'm cumming baby." Both of us climaxed at the same time.

"Lay back on my desk." He ate my pussy so good I

couldn't do anything but scream his name. I didn't care if anyone heard me; this was my man, my heart.

"I love you Iesha." He pulled me up and back on his lap.

"I love you too baby. Are you ok?" I swore his eyes were glassy.

"Yea, I was just thinking of something." I helped him get his clothes back on and cleaned the desk and us both off. Whatever has him upset, will come out eventually.

We were sitting in his office when his mom came in with Summer, Lyric and Jr all in tow.

"Aunty Esha." That's what Jr called me.

"Hey my favorite nephew."

"I'm your only nephew." Did I mention, he's a smart ass?

"Yes, you are. That's why you're my favorite."

"Uncle Darius can we go play basketball later?"

"Yea I'll take you but remember I can't lift you up. So you may be on your own playing unless other kids are out there."

"Ok. What time?"

"Boy, get out of here. I'll let you know when."

"Dag, I was just asking." He said going to sit on the couch with the girls that were watching some show on nickelodeon.

"Iesha, I need to stop by later and I have a surprise for you. I want you to tell your sister she needs to be there also."

"Ok."

"I mean if you can tear those two apart from fucking. I swear they fuck more now than before the shit with the detective bitch kicked off." His mom said laughing.

"Yea it seems like that."

"Ugh, don't think I don't know y'all perverts ain't fucking like rabbits either. I bet y'all were in here fucking before I got here." Darius and I looked at each other and burst out laughing.

"Exactly, that's why both of my daughters are pregnant again. Too much dick in your life will do that to you." I loved Ms. Thomas. She never held her tongue and the shit that came out of her mouth would have you on the floor laughing.

I kept the kids so she could go and get her surprise

ready as she said it.

****

"What's up bitch? Y'all done fucking yet because I got your bad ass son here with me." I yelled in the phone to my sister.

"Whatever. Now that me and my husband are back on track, I have to give him his medicine before we leave the house."

"Come on Ci let me get a little more." I heard him saying the background.

"Tell Cream to cut that shit out. I do not want to hear him begging for some pussy."

"Be quiet. Just make sure my brother is taken care of. We'll meet you at your house in an hour or so."

"Damn nigga you sprung like that?"

"Yup. Bye Iesha." He said hanging up the phone in my ear.

"Don't worry Iesha, I'm strung out on you too." Darius said making me smile.

"It goes both ways baby. I was strung off you the first

137

time you made love to me."

"Mmmmm you were huh?" He asked in between kisses.

"Yea." We stayed a little longer and decided to take the kids out.

We took them to the park for Jr to play basketball and the girls to go on swings.

When we got back to my house, I fed them and gave them all baths; Jr said he was staying over and what he says, goes. That boy was spoiled as hell. I don't know what they were going to do with the next baby.

Darius's mom came over around seven and my sister and Cream came strolling in behind her.

"Hey mommy."

"What's up dad?" He gave Cream a pound like he was grown.

"Mommy, I'm staying over here."

"Yo, what I tell you about telling her what you're going to do instead of asking?" Cream yelled at him.

"I'm sorry dad. Ma, Aunty Esh said I could stay. Is it ok?"

"I'm ok with it but ask your dad."

"Yea go ahead. Don't let me hear you talking like that again."

"Ok. I love you mommy. I'm sorry if I was being mean." She shook her head and gave him a hug.

The one thing they didn't do was allow him to be disrespectful or rude no matter how spoiled he was. Ci Ci was a pushover with him but Jr didn't play when it came to Cream. He told Jr to always respect woman and treat her he way he wanted someone to treat his mom, sister, aunt, cousins and grandma. I was glad he was raising him like that. We needed more men like Cream and Darius in the world. Shit; half of these men are chasing ass to get a quick nut; only to end up with a bunch of kids and diseases.

Ci Ci

We got to my sister's house and Jr got in trouble by his father like he always did. I loved the way James handled him. Whenever I couldn't handle him, I would send him in the room with his father. He would come out and apologize and that would be the end of it. He was only two going on thirteen. I don't know if it was the new daycare, we put him in or what.

I grabbed a banana out the fruit bowl, peeled it and stuck it in my mouth. I noticed Cream was staring at me, so I started sucking the banana like it was his dick.

"Stop playing Ci Ci." He said out loud making everyone look. I shrugged my shoulders acting like I had no idea what he was talking about. He looked at me again, so I continued; he snatched me up and took me in the back bathroom.

"What are you doing Ci Ci?"

"Nothing. I'm just eating my banana." I put it back in my mouth. He threw the banana in the garbage and put his hands in my pants.

140

"Not here James. Shit." I moaned in his ear and grinded on his fingers.

"Nah, you wanna play games, I got something for that ass." He kept going until he felt me explode on his hands.

"Daddy, why was mommy sounding like she was crying in the bathroom? Is she ok?" Jr asked when he opened the door. I grabbed his hand and walked back in the living room.

"That's what y'all nasty asses get. Damn, can you ever take a break?" Darius said. I stuck my tongue out at him and sat next to James.

"Anyway, I have a surprise for you two girls, but I need to tell you to brace yourselves."

"Ma, what are you talking about?" Darius was sitting next to my sister who was on the edge of the couch.

"Before I give it to you, I need to tell you two something." We sat back and waited for her to speak. She seemed nervous.

"The day of Iesha's housewarming party at her condo, I ran into your mom. As you can see neither one of us were

141

happy about that." She went on to apologize for fighting her that day but neither one of us cared.

"Years ago, after the guys dad passed away, I met your father in the grocery store. He was charming and handsome as ever. He and I exchanged numbers and went out on a few dates. I didn't find out he was married until your mom showed up at the restaurant one day screaming and hollering about me being a home wrecker." My mouth dropped because my mother always acting as if she weren't ghetto like that in front of us.

"I was pissed at your father and wouldn't speak to him for months. Fortunately, we reconnected at the mall and that's when he explained to me the marriage situation with your mom. You girls didn't know this, but he and your mom were legally separated but she refused to move out the house.

He showed me the paperwork and I made the decision to continue seeing him. People may feel like it wasn't right, but I saw it in writing. Your mom showed up on plenty of our dates showing her ass and each time, your dad would snatch me up and we would find somewhere else to go." I couldn't believe my mother. She did some crazy shit but damn.

"Anyway, all he ever talked about was his girls and how he loved them so much but gave Iesha a little more attention because her mom hated her. The reason she hated Iesha so much was because she felt he spent too much time with her and not your mom."

"What?"

"Believe it or not she was deathly jealous of Iesha. She put her in a stove one day and your dad found her just before she turned it on. On more than one occasion she left her at school late, hoping child protective services would take her away saying she was unfit. The list goes on and on about the shit she did. When Darius told me what she did at the hospital, I knew it was her jealousy and rage showing on her again."

"Wait! So you're telling me you were sleeping with their dad?" Darius asked her. Iesha had tears running down her face. I went over and hugged her.

"Yes, we were in love and planned on getting married. You guys never knew about him because you were out doing your own thing. He served her with divorce papers and signed a month-to-month lease on a small apartment until everything was final. The very next day, their father started falling ill. Your mom took him to the doctor where they informed him he had cancer. I kept telling him to get a second opinion because no one gets sick that quick and then ends up with cancer the next day. He was against it and kept saying he didn't need one. I knew all about the beatings that she started giving Iesha once he couldn't get out the bed." I shook my head because it was crazy listening to this woman say she knew my father.

"One day your father called me when your mother went on some vacation. I mean who goes away when their husband's dying? Anyway, he asked me to take him to the doctors because he thought it was time for him to die. I took him to my own doctor and come to find out he never had cancer and the reason he was sick was because your mom was giving small doses off arsenic." I covered my mouth as the tears were now falling from my eyes.

"My mom was killing my dad slowly and we never knew." I asked in between cries. Thank goodness we put the kids upstairs before she spoke. Cream came over and took me in his arms.

"Girls look. That's still your mom but she hated that your father didn't want her anymore. The fact his love was stronger for his daughters and another woman drove her crazy. Ci Ci your mom tried to shield you away from all the shit she did to your sister and your father, that's why she kept you in after school programs, and any other activities. Your father loved both of you very much and he never had a favorite. He just tried to protect Iesha because Ci Ci didn't need it. I have someone who can explain all of this better than me." She went to open the door and there stood my father looking handsome as ever.

"Oh shit." Darius said as he caught Iesha when she passed out.

"Daddy." I ran up hugging him. The way he squeezed me let me know he missed us just as much.

"But how? I saw you in the casket."

"Hold on let me check on your sister." He went over there and helped his mom fan her. Cream brought a wet rag out the bathroom and his mom ran it over her face. A few minutes later, she opened her eyes. Her head was on Darius lap.

"What happened?"

"Baby you passed out."

"Darius, I thought my dad was here." Just as she said that my dad stood over her. She sat up and ran her hand down his face.

"Daddy." When he shook his head yes, she jumped in his arms.

After the initial shock wore off, he started telling us everything our mom did. He told us he faked his death to get away from her and had been staying in Florida in one of the vacation houses he had out there. He had to stay away until he found a way to get back at my mom. He knew everything that went on with her trying to kill my niece.

He came out here to see his grandkids and move in with their mom. They had been discussing it for a while and there's no better time like the present.

Iesha and I didn't want our dad to leave but he promised to see or call us everyday. I didn't doubt him either because James mom was around us just as much.

"Can you believe my dad is alive?" I asked James while he was in the shower.

"Nah, your mom is really crazy." He came in the room and put his pajama pants on. I climbed in the bed with him and laid under his arm. He flicked the TV on and put on Netflix.

"Ugh, you know if they get married that makes you my sister."

"Oh don't start. But if that's how you're going to look at it then we need to separate now. I mean no more medicine for you." I looked up at him.

"Don't play with me. You know sister or not that's for my mouth only." I smiled and enjoyed the movie with my husband. I felt like my life was complete now that my dad was back, Darius was ok, and my marriage was stronger than ever.

I do admit that sometimes I miss my mom and wonder if she ever made it. The last I heard, she was in a coma from when Darius threw her out the hospital room. The damage to her brain was extensive and she was basically a vegetable. They couldn't pull the plug on her because it was a small sign of brain activity. Oh well, I guess we'll never know and after

finding all that shit out who cares.

Darius

The whole shit with the Iesha and her dad had me looking differently at our situation. Her mom was a grimy ass bitch and I wish she would come for her again if she ever woke up from that coma I put her in. I had my gun ready this time.

Iesha and I were on our way to Ci Ci's house for dinner. Her father didn't want to step foot in their old house but she wanted to show him all the changes she made. Evidently, there were so many, the only thing that was the same was the outside structure. She even had that painted.

"Wow Cecilia. You did a great job. You sure you don't want to go into interior design?"

"No. I like my job even though my husband doesn't want me to work."

"And she shouldn't. She doesn't need to work, and she has access to all my money so she already knows what time it is." My brother said chiming in.

"From the sound of it, neither one of my daughters have to work."

"No they don't. But both of them are independent."

"Yea, those are my daughters." We finished looking around and sat down to eat.

Ci Ci made so much food we couldn't even have dessert. The kids were running around the house playing while we sat in the living room. I glanced at Iesha who was sitting close to her dad. I stood up and stepped in front of her. She stared at me like I was crazy. Cream helped me bend down in front of her on one knee. She gasped and covered her mouth.

"Baby, you know I love you and there's no other woman I would rather have in my life then you. I believe God made you just for me and I want you to take my last name. Will you marry me?" She shook her head quickly and let me wipe the tears from her eyes.

"Yes baby. 100 times yes." She let me place the 7-carat ring on her finger. I could've gotten her a bigger one, but I always heard her speak on how some woman had rings that were too gaudy. She felt like they were showing off how much money they had and there was no need for it.

I stood up and she jumped in my arms making me fall back on the loveseat.

"Oh my God are you ok baby?" She asked looking nervous.

"I'm good. As long as you're happy."

"I'm very happy. I love you." She put her hand out and observed the ring from a distance. You know the shit women do when they get one.

"It's about damn time." Ci Ci said giving me a kiss on the cheek.

"You know how difficult her ass is. I had to make sure she was ready."

"Congratulations brother." Cream gave me a hug. My mom and their dad did the same.

"Aunty you getting married to uncle Darius?"

"Yea man. Are you going to walk down the aisle with the ring for me?"

"Yup. Daddy, are you and mommy getting married?"

"Baby, we're already married." Ci Ci answered him.

"Oh. Ok well can I wear a suit?" He kept asking question after question. I pray my daughters don't ask that many questions at that age.

We went to Iesha's house instead of mine. I was getting better everyday but I didn't want to be away from her. She would stay at my house, but all Summer's things were here. She took the mail out the box and Summer stayed close to me walking in.

"Oh God." She dropped an envelope and paper in front of her. I had Summer pass it to me. It was a bunch of letters from magazine clippings put together.

"I'm coming for you bitch and I'm killing you, that kid and any others you have."

She started crying hysterical. I pulled her in my arms and told her everything would be ok.

I called my brother and told him we had to have a meeting with our team. We were still looking for Monster and now someone else is coming for my family. I didn't want to come out of retirement, but it looks like I don't have a choice.

Cream

"I'm sorry James I didn't mean to." Were the last words to leave that detectives mouth before I splattered her brains on the living room floor. I told her not to come for my wife and she didn't listen.

I almost lost it when I saw her pointing that gun in Ci Ci face. All it took was one false move and she could've killed her. I was proud of my wife and how she handled the situation inside the police station.

When my mom brought her dad to the house that was one for the record books. Who tries to kill their husband and daughter over bullshit?

I'm glad my wife and I are back together but little does she know I moved her and my sons' stuff back to my house. We were no longer doing that back and forth nonsense.

She just had my daughter who we named Patience. Don't ask me why but that's what she wanted. My brother had his twin boys two months ago. One he named after him and the other after me. We always said when we had our kids the second son would be named after one another.

"Daddy is mommy going to forget about us now that Patience is here?" I took my son in the room with me to see his mom. Her face lit up when she saw him.

"There goes my little man. I've missed you honey." She told him.

"I missed you too mommy but you saw me this morning."

"I know but I still miss you when you leave."

"What about daddy do you miss him too?"

{Daddy knows what's up and how I miss him." She licked her lips at me; making me adjust my jeans.

My daughter was a month old and I still had to wait another two weeks to get some. I loved my wife and my kids but this six-week shit is bullshit. Her pussy closed up right after my daughter came out. After the pain and stitches resolved she should be allowed to have sex right away. Who made that damn rule up anyway?

"And mommy knows how much I miss her too." I

pretended like I was fucking her from the back using the dresser. Jr went to turn around, but she caught him.

I went downstairs to check the mail and saw an envelope with no return address on it addressed to Ci Ci. I opened it up an out fell the same type of letter my brother told me Iesha got.

"I see you had another baby by that nigga. Don't worry I'll be by to visit you." Is what the letter said? I didn't even bother getting mad because whoever it was didn't know that Iesha an Ci Ci went everywhere we did and if not, they were together or with my mom and their dad. We put them on some buddy system type shit just in case.

I tossed that shit, dropped her and the kids off at my moms and went to the office. We were hosting s party for some up and coming rapper from Paterson tomorrow night and Darius, Louis and I were making sure inventory was done, stocked up on everything and any paperwork that needed to be handled was done as well.

"James there's someone to see you in your office." I heard Damien say in his fake ass dramatic voice. I don't let my staff call me by my first name, but Ci Ci asked me to let him because that was her friend.

I walked in my office and it was pitch dark except for some candles that were lit throughout. I saw rose petals on the floor leading all over with no destination. Soft music was playing in the air. I shut the door and locked it. The office chair turned around and there sat my wife in a red see through teddy with the pussy part out. The stockings stopped at her thigh and the red bottom heels she had on topped the entire outfit off.

"Damn you did all this for me?" I asked sitting on my desk in front of her.

"No. I did all this for my husband. I wonder if he likes it." She unbuckled my jeans and pulled them and my boxers down.

"I love everything you do… do…do… for me. Oh shit." I was stuttering as she had me lost in the moment with my dick in her mouth. After I came, she bent over on the desk and begged for me to fuck her.

"You got two weeks baby." She moved her ass closer and put her fingers in between her legs to please herself. I

156

watched and stroked myself at the same time.

"You want me to make love to you?"

"I don't want James to make love to me today. I want Cream to fuck me."

"Oh, you want Cream to come out and play huh? Bring that pussy here."

"You better fuck me right now Cream and make me cum hard." I grabbed her waist and rammed into her so hard she screamed out.

"Yes baby just like that. Fuck me." I smacked her ass and lifted one leg up to dig deeper.

"Harder baby. Oh yes. Like that." The harder I pumped, the more she screamed.

I turned her over and laid her down on my desk. I put my hands on her ankles and spread her pussy open as far as it could go. I started off slow and soon felt my dick falling deeper inside. She was so wet, I really felt like I was drowning in her.

"Fuck me back Ci Ci."

"I can't Cream. I'm about to cum. Oh my God baby. It

157

feels so good I can't stop cumming." She wasn't lying either. Her pussy juices continued leaking out making me cum inside her at the same time.

"Let me taste you baby." I told her after we caught our breath.

"Nope. Only my husband James gets that privilege. Right now, you're Cream and I just want to be fucked all over this office." I laughed at first until I saw she was serious. But I gave her exactly what she wanted.

We fucked on my desk again, the couch, floor and in the bathroom. She's about to be mad but trust and believe Cream just got that ass pregnant again.

My wife and I laid naked on the couch while I ran my hands through her hair.

"I can't imagine another man touching you."

"And you shouldn't because it won't ever happen." She lifted up to kiss me when we heard a knock on the door.

"Who is it?" I don't know why I thought the person could hear me with the music in my office and downstairs. I had her take her stuff to get dressed in the bathroom. I threw all my clothes back on and turned around to make sure she was outta sight before I unlocked it.

"What's up?"

"Damn what you got going on up in here?" Darius and Louis asked walking over the rose petals. Ci Ci opened the door and came out in some jeans and a t-shirt.

"I should've known. You know you probably pregnant again right?" Louis said making her blush.

"I better not be. My husband would be mad because I just fucked Cream all over this office."

"I can't stand y'all." Iesha said walking in.

"Where are you coming from?"

"Darius office."

"Bitch you got some nerve when you came in with me to do the same thing. Oh hell no. Maria don't tell me you just came out Louis office." She laughed and tried fixing her clothes.

"Ok what's going on up here? Ugh uh, all y'all heffas up here getting dick and I'm downstairs working. Y'all ain't shit." Damien said rolling his eyes and went back down. We all

159

laughed our ass off.

"And where you been Maria? We haven't seen you in a minute."

"I went to visit my grandmother on her deathbed."

"Oh, I'm sorry to hear that." Iesha and Ci Ci both said.

"Yea, but she died peacefully. She left me a large insurance policy, but I gave it to my mom for her and my brothers. Me and my man have money and what my grandmother left, I can spend in a day." They hi fived each other.

"You ready to go?" I asked my wife. We all ended up leaving at the same time. I had to be up early so we could set up for the party.

We picked the kids up and went home. Ci Ci's phone rang, and it was the ADT people who told her someone broke into her house. We drove over there, and Iesha and Darius came in behind us. She got the same call. We explained to the cops who we were and he said someone broke the glass on the back door.

The person came in and spray-painted the word *bitches*

on a few of the walls. There was urine and feces on some of the floors and the house smelled like gas as if they were waiting for someone to light a match.

"We fingerprinted as much as we could. Hopefully, the person didn't wear gloves and are in the system." The officer said before shaking our hands and leaving.

"Ci Ci you do know you're not ever coming back to this house again."

"I know baby. Let me just grab some things and the rest can get donated to charity. Iesha, I'm just going to put it on the market." She shook her head at her. I knew they wanted to keep the house in the family, but someone doesn't want them to be happy. First thing tomorrow, I was getting someone to place cameras in the property to make sure no one comes back around.

"Are you ok?" I asked her after she finished breast-feeding my daughter. I didn't want her to do that, but she wanted to try it. The nurse kept telling her it was best for the baby, so she tried it out.

At first, she said it hurt too bad but then she got used to

it. She already started pumping bottles for the next two days. Her breasts were always leaking so she would freeze some of the milk. She planned on drinking tomorrow night, so she made sure there was enough.

"Yea, I'm fine baby. I just don't know why someone would try and break in there. Not once in all these years has that ever happened. Thank goodness the kids and I are back home."

"Right where you belong."

Iesha

Tonight, was the party the guys were having for a rapper and it was going to be super crowded. My dad and Darius mom said they would keep the kids so we could all be together at the club.

Me, Ci Ci and Maria got up early this morning to get our hair and nails done then we went shopping. The guys didn't want to go too early but they did want to be there before the guy.

They had a red carpet lined up, a few newspaper people, I thought I saw the chick that wrote for the shade room, then the one for industry on blast. There was also a guy who took photos inside the club for people to go online and buy.

Damien rolled in with us because he begged them to give him off for the night. The bartenders had people lined up for drinks at all three spots; and the VIP sections were all taken except two. One was for us and the other one was for the rapper and his huge entourage we knew he was coming with.

Rappers always came with at least thirty niggas and ended up with thirsty bitches up there too.

It was a little after midnight and the dude came in and the bitches went crazy. We were watching from VIP how they ran over but security pushed most of them away. He came up to our section introducing himself and a few of his boys.

"Esh is that Sky over there?" Maria asked pointing down at one of the bars. She was standing there with two skank looking chicks. There dresses barely covered their ass and their cleavage was busted out of the top.

"Yea, that's her." I watched her closely as she and those chicks stared up in our direction. Darius came over grabbing me from behind, kissing in my neck.

"I'm dicking you down tonight baby girl. That ass looking real good."

"You know you got that baby." I said with my arms around his neck.

"Did you know Sky was coming here? Not that it's a problem but who are those bitches she's with?"

"I have no idea, nor do I care. All I'm worried about is my fiancé screaming my name later."

"You're such a freak baby but I love it." He smacked me on the ass and went to sit with Cream and Louis.

It was a little after one and the party was still live. Cream and Darius walked down to the bar area to see if they needed anything. Louis went to tell the DJ the guy was getting ready to go on.

"What's your name?" I asked the rapper. I got tired of calling him that.

"I'm Fetty and this is my boy Monty."

"Oh ok. Well good luck on stage."

"Are you seriously telling me you don't know who we are?"

"I'm sorry. I don't listen to rap or watch videos. I barely have the radio on; please don't be offended."

"You don't know the song Trap Queen or 679?"

"Yea but the guy that sings that has an eye missing." He lifted the dreads from over his eye.

"Oh shit. My bad. I wasn't even paying attention. Hell yea I know those songs." He smiled and gave me a hug.

"It's ok ma. If you were my woman, I wouldn't want you watching niggas on TV either. Matter of fact come on stage with me and bring your girls." I shrugged my shoulders and went to the stage with Ci Ci and Maria following.

They introduced him on the stage. He started rapping and singing the trap queen song and I swear everybody in the crowd knew every damn word. Ci Ci was singing along with Monty on the 679 song. She loved when he said, *"They be like Monty can you be my baby daddy, I'm like yea."* Then she loves when he says *"You don't want no sauce no A1."* She thought those were the best versus to the song.

The guys weren't paying us any mind as we stood up there dancing and chilling with them. Believe it or not, they weren't disrespectful and when they called some chicken heads up there, they made sure they wasn't on no rah rah shit because we were up there.

Of course you know Fetty and Monty wanted to see a twerking contest. Darius looked straight at me with the face

166

saying I better not. I was mad as hell because I knew I could twerk better than some of these chicks.

They started mingling in the crowd afterwards and ended up at the bar talking to the guys. It was crazy because he was this big-time rapper; yet he was still chilling with his fans. A lot of celebrities usually sit in VIP and watch from above which in some situations you don't have a choice.

Everything was going fine until I saw Sky and those chicks standing next to Darius and Cream. One had her hand on Cream's chest and the other one was leaning her ass into Darius. I pointed that shit out to Ci Ci and it was ball game. Maria put a braid in her hair and followed behind us.

"Cream how about you and I exchange numbers and hook up at a later time." You heard the one girl say.

"Nah, I'm good. You see my wife don't play that shit. I suggest you keep it moving." He told her pulling Ci Ci in front of him.

"Darius it feels like you're happy to see me." She said grabbing his dick. I twisted that bitch arm back so fast. She snatched it back but stood in front of him with her arms folded.

167

"You're just going to let her dance in front of you like that and then grab your dick Darius. Where is the fucking respect?" I was beyond pissed.

"And Sky why would you bring these two ho's with you and why didn't you tell them they were taken?" She put her hands up in surrender and backed away from the bar.

"Iesha that shit happened real quick. I didn't even get time to react."

"Real quick huh? How is that, when I saw her grinding her ass on you from VIP?"

"Don't be like that baby."

"Don't be like that? Well it looks like I need to be; being though she got your fucking dick hard doing it." I pointed down and his shit was poking out. That bitch stuck her tongue out just a little to make one of those seductive faces.

"You know any other time I would be jumping all over this bitch for that shit but there's no need. It's obvious you wanted it so be my guest and take her home."

"You don't mean that shit Iesha." Maria said.

"No, he can because the way I see it, is that he wants to know what that dirty ass pussy feels like if she can get arise out of him like that."

"I'm not saying you're wrong for feeling the way you do but don't invite another woman into your bedroom when you know you won't be able to handle it. I get it; you're mad but that's pushing it." Maria spoke in my ear. I folded up my arms and waited for his response. He stood there looking stupid as hell.

"Come on Darius. She just gave us permission to go so lets go." She said in his ear and rubbed on his chest. He was staring at me trying to read me. When this nigga walked out the club with her, I was done. I went up to the office, got my stuff and went to leave. He blocked the doorway so I couldn't leave.

"Aren't you leaving with that ho?"

"Calm your little ass down. Ain't nobody leaving with that bitch, and no we did not exchange numbers. I don't know what the fuck is going on but I do know you better not ever invite me to fuck another bitch. Yea, she danced in front of me

169

and I'm not going to lie; it felt good and got my dick hard. What do you expect; her ass was barely covered? You know after everything we've been through, I'm not fucking no other woman. I just asked you to be my wife." He was yelling at me and taking my clothes off at the same time.

"Get off me Darius. She still should've never been that close to you." He had me bent over on the couch with my leg lifted.

"You're right and I'm sorry. I was talking and not paying her any mind until she got too close. By that time, you were already in front of me."

"Ahhh." I screamed as he forcefully entered me.

"Darius, I wasn't even ready."

"I don't care. You need to learn that you're the only one that will ever get this dick. Don't ever question me like that or try to embarrass me in front of anyone." He was fucking the shit out of me. I came back to back and he was still going.

"I'm sorry baby. Do you forgive me?" I was bouncing up and down on his dick, hard then slow.

"I don't know. You have to make your dick cum first."
I squeezed my pussy tightly around his dick and within seconds he came.

"Do you forgive me now?"

"Yes. Now you owe me something else for making a scene."

"I thought I just gave you what you wanted."

"Nah, that was for running your mouth. Causing a scene is different."

"Oh yea. What is it that you want?"

"Speak into that microphone baby girl." I gave my man what he wanted.

By the time we went back down to join everyone the club was clearing out and the party was in the streets. I noticed Sky looking scared and walking back towards the club; I yanked her ass up.

"What the fuck Sky?" Darius looked at me shaking his head.

"Listen Iesha, you know I don't want no problems. I'm just doing what I was told."

"What you were told?"

"Yea." She answered.

"What do you mean?" I asked and waited for her to answer.

"Some lady saw me at the park with Lyric yesterday and told me that if I didn't do what she said, she was going to kill my baby." She started crying. I felt bad for her but I wanted to know what happened. Ci Ci and Maria walked over to us.

"She said some shit regarding this party and she couldn't stand the guys that owned the club or their women. She wanted me to bring these two girls in and have them come on to the guys. All I had to do was point them out and they would handle the rest."

"I should beat the shit out of you." Maria pulled me back when I was just about to swing on her.

"Why didn't you say something Sky? That's Darius's daughter too and you know damn well he wouldn't allow anything to happen to her."

"I know but I was scared."

172

"You were scared so you allowed these two bitches to get close to our men instead of saying something? Get the fuck out my face." Darius came over when he saw Maria holding me. I told him what happened and then Louis and Cream had to hold him back from getting to her.

"Get you and my daughter's shit together. Amir is going to take you down to your mom's house in Maryland. You'll be safe there until we find out what the hell is going on.

"Oh, she said she's coming when you least expect it." I ran around Maria and punched her ass in the mouth. I went to hit her again and Darius had me up in the air.

"You stupid bitch. You got this bitch out here telling you she after us and you don't say two words." Darius put me down while Cream handed her some tissue for her busted lip.

"I hope she does get you. I hate you for taking my man. You don't deserve him and Lyric needs her father. Come on Darius." He looked at her like she was crazy.

"Come on Darius. What the hell is that about?" I asked and she started laughing.

173

"Oh, he didn't tell you." She wiped the blood off her mouth.

"That's right bitch, when you slept with your ex, guess whose shoulder he cried on and guess who's pussy he fell in and he's been in it; even after you got back together."

"When was the last time you were with her?" He wouldn't say anything.

"Tell her yesterday right in your office. That's right bitch. We fucked quite a few times and guess who's pregnant again. Yup by your man." I looked at Darius with the most disgusting look.

"You let me fuck you in that office when I came there yesterday knowing you fucked her that morning? Never mind that I just fucked you up there an hour ago."

"That ring he gave you is his guilt eating away at him. You walk around this motherfucker like your pussy is golden. Ha, the joke is on you because this pussy between my legs is where he really wants to be. Tell her Darius."

"Shut up Sky."

"No don't tell her to shut up now. All the shit she just said and you're just now telling her to shut up. You should've stopped that a long time ago. Now who's getting embarrassed?" Everybody was just about gone but the few stragglers that were left stood there in shock.

"I'll be in Maryland with your daughter waiting for you. Oh, and Iesha, he said those twins were an accident and that he didn't want to have any more kids by you." I went to run after her, and Louis grabbed me.

"You can beat my ass all you want it still won't change the fact that I have his heart." I could feel my eyes getting glassy; yet, I refused to allow that bitch or this nigga to see me cry.

"Iesha let me talk to you." I punched him square in the nose and went walking down the street. Maria pulled up next to me in her BMW truck. I jumped in and we left. I wasn't worried about my sister because Cream would never allow anything to happen to her. I knew it was late but I wanted my babies. I stopped by his mom's house and my dad helped me put them in my car that I left there.

"Are you ok Iesha?" I cried in my dad's arms. I missed him so much, but I didn't want to tell him the man of my dreams had been playing me all along. I needed to get away. I kissed my dad on the cheek and told him I would be in touch, and to tell my sister I loved her.

I got in my car with no destination. I was thankful my kids slept the entire ride. By the time I stopped at a hotel I was in Virginia some fucking where. I was glad I had a few hundred dollars in my purse. I rented the room and the kids and me stayed the night.

"Daddy I'm safe."

"Thank goodness. That boy came right after you left. What the hell is going on?"

"Nothing daddy. I need a favor. I just want you to answer with yes or no. I love Ms. Thomas but I know she'll tell him where I am."

"Anything."

"Daddy, can I stay at the vacation house in Florida?"

"Yes. I love the flowers out there."

"Thank you. What color flowers?"

176

"Red." That was his way of telling me there was a key under the red flowerpot. My dad and I played guessing games like this all the time when I was young. I promised to call him when I was settled. He was going to have all my stuff packed up and sent down to Florida.

I know it seems like I'm running but if he wants to be with someone else, I'm looking at it as a fresh start.

Cream

"Yo, what the fuck D? Please tell me you haven't been fucking that girl and got her pregnant again." I asked him as he paced around our living room. Ci Ci was so mad at him she wanted to fight him herself. Her phone rang and she got it off the table to see who it was.

"Hey Maria. No, we haven't heard from her but I'm sure she's ok. Yea, I'll call you when I hear from her." She hung the phone up kissed me before going upstairs. I knew her sister would call her at some point and she probably didn't want to be around him when she did. Darius sat on the couch with his head back and closed his eyes.

"What were you thinking? And with her again. Are you in love with Sky?" I asked waiting to see what he would say.

"Yes; I don't know." Was all he said? I just sat there thinking of how bad he fucked Iesha up and how she must be feeling. To find out your man has been cheating on you, got the same chick pregnant again he cheated on you with and is still fucking her, has to hurt. I didn't know what to say because he was stupid.

"I don't know. I was hurt when she slept with her ex. I went home and asked Sky would she ever cheat on me and she told me no and how she was still in love with me. I went by the bar and came home drunk. I was in the shower and the next thing I know, I had her legs behind her head. It went on for a few weeks and I started catching feelings for her. She has my daughter too and she started staying at the house more. I came home to home cooked meals, back rubs, and sex. I mean what more could I ask for. I started staying at Iesha's house but I didn't stop fucking Sky."

"Then why did you go back to Iesha? Why ask her to marry you?"

"I was being selfish. I didn't want her to be with anyone else. Sky was ok with what was going on."

"Well I guess she wasn't because she sure as hell let everything out tonight."

"I know."

"So what, you were just going to marry her like you didn't have Sky pregnant at home waiting for you?"

"I wasn't thinking that far ahead. Yo, how do you and Ci Ci keep your relationship going? What's holding you two together?"

"Nigga, that's my heart. I knew when I found her, that she was the one that's why I wasn't in a rush to sleep with her."

"Yea, but you cheated on her and she still took you back."

"What I did was for her and she didn't just take me back. Do you remember she left me for months? She wouldn't speak to me unless it was about Jr. You think a nigga didn't cry over that shit. I cried a couple times over my wife leaving me. I broke CiCi; something I vowed never to do to her." I shook my head thinking about it.

"The days I saw her sitting outside the club crying or the time she was pulled on the side of the road tore me up. It took a lot of begging, pleading and praying for her to take me back and I swore on my kids, I would never allow my wife to experience that kind of pain from me again. It took her a minute but she's starting to trust me again and I make sure I let her know everyday, how much I love her and that no one will ever come in between us again."

"That's the kind of love I have for Iesha. I just wanted to explain what happened, but I can't find her. Yes, I'm think I'm in love with Sky but I'm still in love with her too."

"I don't know what to tell you because I can guarantee you lost her for good this time." He got up off the couch gave me a hug and left. I made sure the alarms were on and went to check on my wife who was on the phone crying.

"Is that your sister?" I whispered taking my clothes off. She shook her head yes. I kissed her lips then jumped in the shower. When I got out, she was off the phone.

"Baby how could he do that to her?" I hugged her tight and kissed the top of her head.

"I don't know baby. I don't know." We watched a little TV before we both dosed off.

Ci Ci and I didn't get up until after one. She made us some breakfast while we waited for her dad to bring the kids

181

over. I spoke to my mom who said she was on her way to my brother's house to see what was going on."

"Hey Mr. Barnes, how are you." I said opening the door.

"Hey son. How's my other daughter?"

"Hey daddy, where's mommy?" I guess my mom stopped by after all. CiCi called my mother mom all the time.

"Hey, she's in the kitchen. I'll take Patience from you." I took her out the seat and she opened her eyes.

She resembled her mother so much, and there was no way she was ever dating. Mr. Barnes sat down, and my wife told him in detail what happened last night. He shook his head in disappointment but said he wouldn't judge but he wasn't happy about how he treated Iesha.

After they left, we got dressed and took Jr. to sky zone. He wanted his cousins, Summer and Lyric to come but we told him they weren't home. They were growing up together, so this separation was going to be hard for him. There were so many damn kids here, I left Patience with Ci Ci and walked around watching my son.

"Excuse me." I heard a voice say and I looked up to see that chick from the bar who was rubbing on me. I looked for my wife to see if she saw what was going on.

"Hey it's the sexy man I got paid to come on to. Now that I see you outside of the bar, you are sexy as fuck. Are we ever going to exchange numbers? I bet I can show you some things your wife can't." And she hit the floor before I could answer.

Ci Ci walked over when she saw her and parked my daughters' stroller next to me. She hit the woman so hard she was laid out on the floor. I grabbed my sons' hand and put my daughter in the car. I was mad because my wife was still inside, and I couldn't leave my kids. She walked out a few minutes later with the bitch behind her.

"I apologize for coming on to you and disrespecting your family." I looked down and my wife had a gun poking at her side. I nodded my head and she walked off.

I yanked Ci Ci's ass up and made her get in the car. We rode home silent because I didn't want Jr. to hear us arguing. I told him to go in his room and watch a movie. I took Patience up to her room.

"Are you crazy? Who has a damn gun in Sky Zone where it's nothing but kids?"

"I'm sorry but I started carrying it everywhere since Iesha got that letter." I grabbed her arm and pulled her close to me.

"Baby, I'm not going to let anything happen to you. As far as that woman or any other woman goes, you never have to worry about that."

"I know James. It's just we don't know who is after us and whoever she is, she's trying to break us up. James I can't take you cheating or leaving me."

"She's just trying to get in your head. I'm not messing around and you know I'm not leaving. Don't let what's going on with your sister get to you either. What we have and share is different and stronger than what they did. Know that my entire being belongs to you and only you?" I rubbed the back of her head and told her to go take a bath. I had to find this woman quick before she destroyed my family.

184

Darius

I've been drinking everyday for the past six months when Iesha left me. Sky and Lyric were back here with me but all she and I did was argue. She blamed me for not keeping her safe from Iesha, but she ran her mouth. She knew the type of person my ex was; yet, she thought letting our secret out wasn't going to piss her off.

The night Iesha left, and I talked to my brother, he put a lot of shit in prospective. I did love both of them but I after I thought about it, I was only in love with Iesha. The entire month Sky was in Maryland with her mom I didn't call or go see her. I just sent her a text asking about my daughter. Every time she called, I hit ignore or sent her a message saying I was busy and would call her back. I didn't even ask her to come home; she was here one day I came in from the club. I haven't touched her since that night she told everything but she was now exactly six months pregnant; which means she probably got pregnant the day I fucked her in my office.

I searched high and low for Iesha tho. I tried to track her cell but she got her number changed so much she started using burner phones to call Ci Ci or my mom. I haven't seen my kids and I know my daughter was missing me. I saw a few photos of them from the pictures off Ci Ci phone.

None of the money was touched in her bank account, which meant someone was supporting her. Every time I stopped by the house her sister would roll her eyes and leave the room. I know I fucked up but it didn't have shit to do with her.

"Yo what up?" I said in the phone.

"I'm bringing the kids to your moms. If you want to see them, you can over there."

"Iesha baby don't hang up." I looked at the phone and saw the time still going but she wasn't saying anything.

"Iesha I'm so sorry. I know what I did was foul, and you didn't deserve that." I could hear her sniffling in the background.

"Don't cry baby. I wish you were here so I could hold you and you could see I'm hurting just as bad."

186

"Darius why?" She said into the phone.

"Baby, let me see you when you bring the kids so we can talk face to face please." I didn't give a fuck about begging.

"Who the fuck are you talking to Darius? I know you not on the phone with another bitch and I'm sitting here pregnant with your baby." I looked down at the phone and she hung up. I gave Sky the look of death when I turned around. I grabbed my keys and left. I couldn't stay in the house with her anymore. I wanted to call Iesha back but I didn't have a number to do it.

The next day, my mom called and told me all the kids were there. I dressed Lyric and took her with me leaving her mother right there. I was disgusted looking at her. She didn't wanna do shit but lay on the couch all day. She turned right back into the Sky I first met. I guess a zebra can't change its stripes.

I walked in and Summer came running up to me crying while the boys were playing in their walkers.

"Where's Iesha?" My mom looked at Mr. Barnes.

187

"She dropped them off and left. She didn't say when she was coming back for them but she doesn't want them at your house with Sky. She feels like there's too much hatred Sky has towards her and she doesn't want her doing anything to the kids. You know you're more than welcomed to stay here Darius." My mom said wiping some drool of my son's face.

"How is she going to tell me where I can take my kids?"

"Darius, I agree with her. Sky has hated Iesha since you first started dating her. Iesha has whooped her ass a few times now; she knows she can't get to her and may hurt the kids."

"Fuck that."

"Darius stop. You're mad because she's not here but don't take the kids over there on some petty shit. I would hate for Sky to do something to them and Iesha end up killing her. I suggest you bring some things over here for you and Lyric and spend time with your kids." I listened to what my mom said and after I got out my feelings, I went back to my house to get some things.

"Where are you going and where is my daughter?"

188

"She's staying with me at my mom's house for a few days."

"Oh no she's not. And why are you staying over there when you have a pregnant girlfriend at home?"

"Sky, I never officially made you my girlfriend and I don't have to tell you why I'm staying at my mom's house." I shut the door in her face and left. My mom couldn't stand her, so I wasn't worried about her coming over there.

I went back and drove all the kids over to my brothers so Jr. could see the girls and him and Ci Ci could see the boys again.

"Oh my God look how big they got." Ci Ci said when she opened the door. Cream came and grabbed the other car seat from me.

I walked in the living room and Ci Ci told me Iesha was asleep in one of the bedrooms. I was shocked she gave me that bit of information. I opened the door and went to sit on the bed when I got the shock of my dam life.

"You have to be fucking kidding me. Not again?" Now I understood why she told me where she was. What the fuck?

189

Iesha

I came to Jersey for the weekend to visit my sister and dad; plus drop the kids off to their father. I know it was wrong to up and leave with them but at the time it wasn't. I called him a few times to speak with Summer but then he would call back to back on the phone.

I changed the number a few times but then decided on getting a burner phone. I brought a few $4.99 trac phones and tossed them as soon as I hung who with him. Ci Ci had been showing him pictures too so he could see how they were growing.

My boys were a handful and they were a spitting image of him. They were fraternal and James was a tad bit lighter than Darius Jr. They were crawling and getting into a lot. Summer was just turning two and her tantrums were getting bad. I needed a break and after I dropped them off, I came to my sisters to take a nap.

She was excited to see me but sad at the same time mad because the kids weren't there. Jr came running in my arms and

Patience was getting big. I missed my family and thought about coming back until Darius mom told me Sky was living there with him.

I know it shouldn't bother me, but it does, not only for that reason but she's pregnant again too. I heard kids yelling outside the bedroom door and opened my eyes. I rolled over and let my legs slide off the bed. I stared straight into the eyes of the person I was trying to avoid. He was still sexy as ever standing there in some light blue denim jeans, a white t-shirt, some red Jordan's and a red hat to match.

"What's up Iesha?" He was leaning against the bathroom door.

"Hello Darius." I walked passed him to pee. I already unpacked my stuff, so I brushed my teeth and washed my face. I shut the light off and went to leave the room. He grabbed my arm and hugged me tightly. I wanted to return the gesture, but I couldn't.

"It looks like we're in the same situation again huh?" I backed up laughing.

"Yea I guess so." He said rubbing my stomach. His

touch had me wanting to strip right there. I was horny as hell and I needed to feel him inside me but I stayed strong and moved away from him.

"Iesha you need to come back here. How are you going to take care of four babies?" I shrugged my shoulders and turned the doorknob to walk out.

"Look at me." He moved my hand off the knob and turned me around.

"What?" I stared at him and he had tears coming down just face. He sat down on the bed and started talking.

"Iesha, I'm sorry. I was mad and angry when I caught you with that nigga. I didn't plan on sleeping with her or catching feelings. She was there that night after the bar; I fucked her and instead of stopping, I continued. She started staying at the house making me feel wanted."

"So you didn't feel I wanted you?"

"I'm not saying that. I'm saying my head was all the way fucked up when I caught you coming out that hotel. I'm not ashamed to say you broke my heart Iesha."

"I know Darius and I thought we moved past it when

you came back to me. To find out you were still sleeping with her and even after you got shot, hurts. I was the one that took care of you. I was your woman; not her. I was there; not her. And to think you two pretended like nothing was going on and I was the fool to believe it."

"Iesha, I can't take back what happened. I'm not going to lie, I thought I was in love with her; I did. Shit, I thought I was in love with both of you until you left. When you disappeared I was going crazy looking for you. I didn't care where she was and even though she had my daughter; my main concern was you. I know now without a shadow of a doubt that you are the only woman I'm in love with. And I never told her my sons were conceived by accident. Each time I got you pregnant, is because I wanted to."

"How could you sleep with both of us in the same day at the office?"

"She came by the office to bring me some lunch. I was coming out the bathroom and she was naked on the couch playing with herself. Yes, I could've walked away but I didn't."

"Then why fuck me?"

"Because papers or not, you're my wife. I would never deny sex with you. It may not be right and sound selfish but I'm a selfish man when it comes to you. I don't care what I'm doing, if you need me to make love to you, I will drop everything to do it."

"She has your heart Darius." I felt the tears stinging.

"No she doesn't and you know it. She will always have a place in there because she has my daughter and the one she's pregnant with now, but I never lied when I said you had it. You are the only one that ever had it. She tried to steal it many times but the heart wants what it wants."

"And what does your heart want?"

"You and only you." He said in between kisses.

"Daddy come play with me." Summer said bursting through the door. I was happy because I felt myself falling for him again and I promised myself I wouldn't.

"Hey sleepy head." Ci Ci said and I rolled my eyes at her. I know damn well she told him where I was.

"Don't be like that sis. He had the right to know."

"Whatever." I sat in the living room watching him and

Cream play with the kids. I really was missing my family but only time would tell if I should come back.

CiCi

My sister came to Jersey to visit and allow the kids to be with their dad. I hated Darius for how he played my sister but those were still his kids. It took a lot of convincing to get her to come. She was so hurt over everything, she neglected to tell him she was seven months pregnant. Yea she got pregnant right before he got shot. I swear me, her and their cousin's wife, were running a race on kids. Once one popped out, these niggas were putting more in us.

She and Darius stepped out the room and it looked like he was crying.

"Damn I guess men do cry." I said to my husband.

"Hell yea. Baby, I shed a lot of tears over you." I was caught by surprise when he said that. I saw him cry one time, but I didn't know it happened more than once. He was so strong; who would've thought we were both broken over that shit?

"Hey, do you want to go to the mall?" I asked her. She looked miserable and I know she needed a break. She shook her head yes.

"I'm coming too." Darius said grinning. We left the kids at the house with the nannies and piled up in the car. They got out the car before me and James. I saw Darius take her hand in his and surprisingly she didn't snatch it back.

"What are we here for anyway Ci Ci? You have a shit load of clothes you already don't wear."

"Who said it was for me to buy something to wear out?" I winked my eye and got out. He loved when I wore sexy clothes for him.

"Do I get to pick it out?"

"If you want to see it? I was going to surprise you but hey, I'm down to see what you choose." We stopped in Victoria Secrets first, then Neiman Marcus.

Of course he finally found some bra set that had garter belts and stockings to them. The ass part was missing and there were tassels hanging from the nipples. He picked up a pair of strap up red bottoms to go with it.

"I can't wait to see your sexy ass in this." He whispered in my ear as we walked to the food court. Darius and Iesha were already there. She was at the Japanese place ordering and he was at the table with bags. James told me what he wanted and went over to sit with him. On our way back there were two bitches standing in front of them.

"I'm over this bitch." I put my food down on the table, tapped her on the shoulder and put her on her ass. Her nose was split open and she was out on the floor.

"Ok Ci Ci I see what you working with." Iesha yelled as she pushed the other girl out the way.

"You didn't have to do her like that; we just came over to tell them what was going on."

"Well you should've told us. I told you two before to stay away from our husbands. Yes, husbands bitch. These aren't any street niggas looking for a quick nut. They have families and I'll be damned if you come in trying to destroy that." I was definitely in my feelings over the shit.

"You know what, I'm not telling you shit then. This woman can kill your ass for all I care." She helped her friend get off the ground.

"Bye bitch." Iesha said sticking food in her mouth.

There was an envelope on the floor. James picked it up an opened it.

"Iesha is back in town and I want you to find her man and see if you can get him to fuck you this time. And try something new because for some reason you're not doing a good job. Iesha will fight for him if she still loves him but be careful, her hands are serious.

James is going to be a hard one to get. He is head over heels for his wife. See if you can catch him at the office and slip something in his drink. Get everything on tape and send it to her. She won't allow him to break her twice. We'll link up soon. As usual I'll find you."

"Yo what the fuck?" James was pissed. He passed the letter around. My mouth hung to the floor and Iesha was crying. I'm sure her hormones were all over the place with the pregnancy.

"Let's go." He grabbed my arm and the bags.

"Don't pull on me like that." I said to James and made him slow down.

"I'm sorry baby. I just wanna get outta here. I don't

199

know who this is. Shit isn't safe for any of us right now." We went to the house and saw cop cars sitting outside the house. James and Darius ran inside, and I helped my sister get out.

"I'm sorry Mrs. Thomas, she just walked in with the cops. I was on the phone calling your husband." The nanny said showing me the phone with James number on it.

"It's ok."

"What's going on?" I asked James who was talking to one of the officers.

"Ma'am this woman said this man kidnapped her daughter today."

"What?" Iesha yelled out.

"That's my daughter and these are me and my brothers' kids. Sky what the hell are you doing here and why would you tell the cops I kidnapped her?" Darius was in her face yelling.

"Sir, I need you to back away from her."

"Sky you're on some petty shit. You're only doing this because my sister is here." I told her. She had this devilish grin on her face.

"Yea and this woman attacked me a few months ago."

200

The shock on our faces was evident as the cop was too.

"Ma'am do you have any proof?" She pulled out her phone and showed the cop video footage of Iesha that night at the club.

"That was months ago." I yelled out.

"Well I was forced out of state so I couldn't press charges. Officer I would like to press charges on her now." The officer looked confused but had my sister walk outside so he could handcuff her. We didn't want the kids to see what was going on.

"Sky get the fuck out of my house." I pushed her ass forward since the officers were outside. She looked back grinning.

"Bitch, I will whoop your ass in here." Now that I knew how to fight, I was throwing my weight around like it was nothing.

"That sounds like a terroristic threat. I wonder if I could press charges on you too."

"Go ahead. You think that shit scares me?" It did but I wouldn't give her the satisfaction of knowing that.

"Sky why are you doing this?" Darius asked her grabbing his keys.

"You think I'm going to allow that bitch to get you back? I was the one whose shoulder you cried on when she slept with that other nigga. She left you depressed because she took your kids and you're over here acting like daddy of the year with my daughter."

"Sky those are Lyric's siblings and cousins. When I get back to my house you better be gone."

"You crazy as hell if you think I'm leaving. That's my house. How you even thought you were putting me out without taking my daughter was stupid."

"Just go Darius. Lyric will be fine here."

"She's going home with me, thank you very much."

"When did you become tough? Oh, I see you think because you're pregnant by my brother that no one will lay hands on you? Sky he doesn't want you and the faster you get that through your head the better." James told her and shut the door in her face.

"Give me my daughter before I call the cops back over

202

here." James opened the door back up and stepped in her face.

"Bitch, I wish you would. Lyric is staying here until my brother gets back and he will decide when she comes home. Now get the fuck off my steps before I help you." James stood over her waiting for a response. I swear when he turned into Cream motherfuckers backed up. She waddled her stupid ass down to the car and left.

"Umm I think you need to bring Cream in the bedroom tonight."

"Oh yea. So you don't want me making love to you anymore."

"I always do but sometimes I just want to be fucked and the way you just handled that situation turned me all the way on."

"This is my last time allowing Cream to fuck you, so you better enjoy it."

Cream

I don't know what was going on but it definitely felt like a storm was brewing. The shit with Iesha, my brother and Sky; then someone trying to set me up to cheat on my wife. Whoever this person is must know them well; to know Ci Ci wouldn't take me back if I cheated again, or Iesha will fight for my brother if she still loves him.

I've checked all the security cameras at the old house daily and no one has come back since the break in. This shit was frustrating and making me want to camp out at that chick's house just to see who it was.

My brother came back to the house with Iesha a few hours later and told us how Sky came down to the station and gave them the footage of the video and cried like a baby about missing Lyric. That bitch gave two shits about my niece; she only kept her thinking my brother will stay with her.

"I don't know what type of shit Sky was on but you can bet I'm going to the bottom of it." Darius said going to the door.

"Hold on Darius." Iesha said. Ci Ci and I looked at both of them smiling. They were standing by the door so me and my nosy ass wife went to listen.

"Darius don't go over there bugging out and get yourself locked up. I'm ok and you already told me the charges are going to disappear."

"Fuck that Iesha. That shit wasn't cool at all; then she said I kidnapped my own daughter. I'm about to fuck her up for real." Iesha grabbed him and kissed him. He grabbed her by the waist and they went at it for a few minutes. That was our cue to go back in the other room.

"Do you think they'll get back together?"

"I don't know. Iesha is pretty stubborn and what he did took a toll on her."

"Y'all nosy as hell." She said walking back in the room.

"What?" We both said laughing.

"I know you were standing there listening."

"So are you going to take him back?" Ci Ci asked.

"Damn all we did was kiss. I was trying to calm him down. I don't want him getting locked up."

"Umm hm, why you care?"

"I don't care but the kids would miss him."

"Its ok Iesha if you still love him. I went through the same thing with this fool but what we share is stronger now than before."

"That's right." I said listening and watching TV at the same time.

"Don't get it twisted though. If his ass ever cheats again, I won't be as forgiving and nothing he does will get me back." I know she was telling her that to make sure I didn't fuck up again. She was always saying subliminal shit like I wouldn't know she was talking about me.

"Yea, but Cream messed up once. This nigga keeps messing up."

"Yea and he better not mess up again."

"Girl ain't nobody cheating on you again. Your pussy got me strung and I told you no one was ever taking my spot." I smacked her ass and tickled her on the couch.

"I love you."

"I love you too."

"Ok can we get back to my problem sis?"

"Listen sis, Darius is a good man that keeps making bad decisions. He's probably not used to being tied down but if you love him, then teach him. It's obvious he loves you because he dissed the shit out of Sky soon as he heard you were back in town. I know it's hard forgetting, but you have to forgive him before you can move forward whether it's with him or not. The decision is yours and fuck what everyone else says about it. You are the one that has to wake up with him everyday and if you want to be with him, then do it. But don't hold back because you think people are going to clown you. The world is full of haters so even if he wasn't cheating, they would find a reason to talk."

"I really do love him. I fucked up with Monster and he fucked up with Sky but I don't want to keep taking him back either."

"It's up to you Iesha. Ci Ci can only give you advice on what she went through and how she got past my infidelity. You may or may not be able to and that's fine but if that's what you choose, then kissing and sleeping together is not a good idea either."

"I know."

"You two have to sit down and let each other know what your expectations are before you can think about building a future together again. You'll always be my sister in law regardless." I was being as honest as I could with her.

"Now I'm sorry to be the bearer of bad news but Cream just got here, and he wants his sidepiece upstairs and in that outfit she got from the mall earlier." I gave her a kiss on the cheek and went to fuck my wife who left not too long ago to wait for me.

"Ugh, I swear she's going to end up pregnant again and Patience ain't even one yet."

"Who says she's not already?"

"Are you serious?"

"I don't know but if she's not, she'll be tonight. Cream is trying to take her from her husband."

"Ok, I do not want to hear about y'all freaky roll playing sex capades."

"Good night sis."

"Good night. I'm sleeping down here. You be having my sister screaming too loud for me."

"I know." I winked and went upstairs. Ci Ci was lying back on the bed in that outfit looking sexy as FUCK. Yea Cream murdered that pussy so bad she couldn't even walk the next day.

Darius

"Yo what the fuck Sky?" I slammed the door and found her eating ice cream on my leather couch. I snatched that shit out her hand an tossed it across the room. I didn't care it splattered everywhere. All that mattered was she got my kids mother arrested on some bullshit.

"I was eating that Darius."

"You think I care. Why would you do some dumb shit like that?" She stood up and walked towards me.

"Darius you told me it was going to be us when you slept with me. You promised you were going to try and make it work. Now she's back and you're running back to her. I deserve a chance."

"Sky, I was in a bad place the when I slept with you. And you're right I did promise to try; however, you're back to the old Sky again. You have no motivation, you barely take care of Lyric and you disrespected my mom today when you called asking where Lyric was."

"I didn't mean to but she wouldn't tell me."

"My mom doesn't owe you shit. I can tell you this though; if Iesha finds out you did that, she's coming for you."

"Iesha, Iesha, Iesha. I'm so tired of hearing her name. I wish she would just die already." I put my hands around her throat and threw her ass on the couch.

"I better not ever hear you say no shit like that again about her. Do you hear me?" I could see her turning blue and if it weren't for me remembering the baby in her stomach, I probably would've killed her.

"You're about to kill me over a bitch who don't want you." I heard a loud noise at my back door. I grabbed my gun and put my finger up for Sky to shut up. I looked around the corner an Iesha had her gun pointed straight at Sky.

"You thought you could disrespect my mother in law, get me arrested and sleep with my man and I wouldn't come for you?" Sky had her hands up with tears coming down her face. I went to check my door and she shot the doorknob off. I shook my head laughing and grabbed my water out the fridge. I was in no rush to stop Iesha. Sky brought this shit on herself.

211

"So you're going to let her shoot me while I'm pregnant with your baby?" I just shrugged my shoulders because we found out some disturbing news about her down at the station.

"You know Sky, the craziest thing happened at the station. We were sitting there talking to one of the officers when Darius friend Zach came from the back." It looked like all the blood drained from her face.

"You see Zach and Darius went to school together and After you left being dramatic, he came in off a call and asked us how we knew you when he saw the file. Funny how he didn't even know you had a daughter."

"I can explain Darius."

"Explain what? That you're really eight months and there's no possible way that's my kid."

"Hello Sky." Zach walked in with some chick we assumed was a doctor holding a medical bag.

"Zach let me talk to you." Sky tried pleading her case.

"Nah I'm good. I'm here for one thing, and one thing only."

"What's that?"

"My baby."

"I'm not due yet."

"See that's where you're wrong. My doctor friend here who happens to be my wife, can't have kids. I fucked you and purposely got you pregnant to help us out. You see you're about to die and my baby will be home where he belongs."

"Don't look at me bitch. You did this to yourself." I told her looking at his wife putting something in a needle to shoot her with.

"But you're a cop."

"And you're a ho." I watched the woman step behind her and shoot her in the neck. Sky fell to the floor and the woman started an IV on her and started cutting this bitch stomach opened. I couldn't watch that shit. Zach couldn't either because he and I sat in the kitchen drinking a beer.

I had the clean-up crew outside waiting for her to finish. Twenty minutes later a baby was screaming. We both ran inside and saw his wife holding the baby with tears in her eyes.

"Congratulations you two."

"I'll have the paperwork for you tomorrow. The baby

will have been born from your wife, with all necessary information on it. You know the social security card will take a while." We shook hands and they left with the baby.

"Darius, I can't believe they went through with it."

"Some people will do anything for a baby. Oh and don't underestimate Zach. He's still that same grimy nigga from the hood too. Being in the military and a police officer may have changed him a little, but he still ghetto. I'm going to grab a few things and get all necessary stuff from my safe to take to my brothers. Anything else can be replaced."

"Replaced? Why are you doing that and saying things need to be replaced? And why are you staying with your brother?"

I put a black box upstairs on the floor in the hallway an another one in the middle of the living room. I grabbed her hand, jumped in the car and sped out the driveway.

"Darius what's going on?"

BOOM BOOM!!! The sky lit up like fireworks. She jumped when she heard the noise; then gasped when the house exploded.

"Are you going to tell me why you just blew your house up?"

"It was time that's all." We drove back to my brothers' house in silence. I took my stuff out and she was already at the door going in. Cream was walking down the stairs with Lyric in his arms.

"She was calling out for her mom. I'm going to let you handle that." He passed her to me and Iesha glanced over at me with sad eyes. How do you explain to a two-year-old that her mom is gone and never coming back? You don't I guess. Iesha will be her mother anyway.

"Good night Darius." She went upstairs in the room with the kids and I took Lyric in the room with me. I guess it was her and daddy for the night.

Cream

Today I was taking my wife out on a date. I wanted to remind her why she fell in love with me. I took her to the same place on the beach where I asked her to be my woman.

She came downstairs wearing a white fitted strapless dress with some gold heels and jewelry to match. She looked stunning and I was proud to have her on my arm as my wife.

I could barely keep my hands off her as we sat in the back of the limo I rented. Yes, I rented a limo to make the night extra special. The driver opened the door and we walked in. The waitress sat us at a table overlooking the water.

We spent more time staring at each other and kissing then we talked. It was like we were teenagers on our first date. We ordered our food and talked a little in between. After dinner, I ordered a small brownie cake that was on the menu. When it came out, she started crying.

"Baby, I love you so much. I can never apologize enough for what I put you through. My heart broke each time I saw you cry, and I promise to never allow tears to fall from

your eyes again unless its happy ones. I still want to spend the rest of my life with you. I want to give you the wedding of your dreams and make love to you all night long. Will you marry me again?" I took the ring out the cake and put it on her finger. I stood up and she hugged and kissed me. The entire restaurant was clapping, and a few women had tears in their eyes; they are so emotional. This night was perfect.

We walked in the house and Iesha was standing in the kitchen with one of my nephews. She walked over to see the ring, but Ci Ci went upstairs and told me to follow her. I shrugged my shoulders to Iesha and went to see what she was up too.

I opened the door and there was a banner going across the room that read *Will You Marry Me?* There were silver and white balloons and some Patron on ice for me with a bottle of champagne for her. There was a card and a ring box in the middle of the bed.

"What's this?" I asked picking up the card first. It was and I love you card, but the box held a Platinum wedding band with diamonds in it. She told me to read the inscription. *My life, my world, my everything, Cecilia and James Forever.*

"You were going to ask me to marry you?"

"I was but you beat me to it." She said laughing and stripping at the same time.

"I love it baby. I would've said yes, you know that right?" I grabbed her by the waist and kissed down the back of her neck. We made love all night long.

The next day Iesha and Ci Ci got up to make breakfast for everyone since today was her last day here. Darius seemed to be depressed about her going back but she promised to bring the kids back once a month to see him. I already knew the deal, I was just waiting on her to mention it.

"Daddy are you coming with us?" Summer said eating her eggs.

"Not this time baby girl."

Darius

6 months later....

Iesha came back a week after she left with my kids. She went back to the same house because she never sold it. We were working on getting back together but it wasn't official yet. I was at her house 99 percent of the time and we were both exclusive to one another when it comes to sex. Basically, we were a couple without the title.

"You better be good tonight." Iesha said putting her clothes on. We made love all morning. I think she was trying to get my dick tired.

"You don't have anything to worry about. You gave me enough this morning; I don't need anyone else." I told her.

"That's what I like to hear."

"It is huh?" I asked pulling her closer. I kissed her lips then her neck.

"No more Darius. My pussy is sore."

"Don't you mean my pussy?"

"Whatever."

"When are you going to stop playing and take me back? I've learned my lesson."

"Hmm, you think you deserve my love?" She turned and wrapped her arms around my neck.

"Hell yea."

"I guess I can take you back." I was cheering hard as hell when she said it.

"I swear one fuck up and that's it."

"Don't be so negative. Ain't nobody messing up again. Losing you not once but twice, made me man up and realize there won't be a third time. I love you for teaching me how to love and treat you. I'm glad you didn't give up on me."

"Yea well, that dick and tongue saved you."

"Oh shit Iesha. You got that. Just know I'm going to have you screaming later; sore pussy and all." She smacked me on the arm and went out the room to get Paris our daughter who just turned four months. I had her get the shot in her arm for birth control until Paris turned at least five. We needed a break from popping out babies. Shit; we had five; all 3 and under.

"Ok baby. I'll see you tomorrow at the altar." CiCi and James were having their big wedding tomorrow. She was so excited since the first one was spur of the moment.

"I love you Darius. Please be careful."

"I love you too. What are you worried about?"

"Baby, Monster hasn't been seen or heard from in six months. It's like he dropped off the face of the earth but none of you were the one to do it. I feel like he's lurking around somewhere, and I just want you to watch your back."

"Awww you do love me."

"Boy shut up."

"I'll call you as much as I can or text you. Keep my babies safe too."

I kissed them all and headed out to get ready for tonight. Cream asked Louis and I to both be his best man and tonight was his bachelor party. Yea they were already married but he wanted to give Ci Ci the fairytale wedding. And she was getting just that.

She was having an over the top wedding if you asked me but I'm sure it will be worth it when he sees her coming down the aisle. Louis and I already auditioned a few strippers even though Cream said he didn't want any. What man has a bachelor party with no strippers? At least let the guest enjoy them.

The club was decorated in gold and black, the dude Fetty hit me up and said him and his crew were stopping by and my cousin and some of his people were coming through. All of them were coming in from P.R including my aunt, who I hadn't seen since his overnight wedding.

I was getting ready at Creams house when I heard him yelling on the phone. He came in talking. I waited for him to hang up before I asked what was up.

"Yo someone from the airport saw Monster touch ground this morning and some woman was waiting for him."

"They lost him in traffic but said he was going south on the parkway."

"Ok. At least we know he's in town, so we'll keep an eye on him. Get yourself ready so we could get out of here. It's already after ten."

We picked Louis up who was arguing with Maria about touching on niggas at the bachelorette party.

"I better not smell no niggas when I get home."

"And I better not smell any bitches either." She said mushing him in the head. She stuck her finger up at us and shut the door.

We pulled up to the club around 11 and the line was around the corner. Cream didn't wanna close the club just for a bachelor party. He felt the more niggas, the more money.

VIP was packed with Fetty and his crew along with us and a few other people. It was time to go downstairs for the festivities to begin.

"For all of you that didn't know my brother Cream is getting married tomorrow." You heard a few chicks suck their teeth and some dudes say good luck.

"Anyway, we are gonna show him a good time tonight. So men and women if you're interested; get ready to make it rain." Louis said on the microphone getting people amped up.

The song *what you twerking with* came on and about

twenty strippers came out doing the damn thing. There was ass and tits everywhere. Chicks were popping their pussy on the floor, on each other, doing upside down tricks in front of dudes and Cream just sat there smiling. I knew he wanted to touch but I also knew he wasn't trying to lose Ci Ci again, and with all these cameras and videos; that was his best bet.

When the clock struck twelve a huge cake was brought out to the middle of the floor. The song *Motivation* came on by Kelly Rowland and the top opened. Some badass chick came out. She wore an all-white cat suit. The stomach was cut out and holding itself together by some strap thing. She wore white red bottoms and a clear mask that looked like it belonged in the Purge movie. Her hair hung down to the middle of her back and her ass wasn't huge but it was big enough to smack and jiggle. She walked over to Cream seductively to the song and sat down on his lap in a straddling position.

"Yo if I wasn't married, I would snatch that ass up and take her in one of y'all offices." Miguel said sipping on his beer. I shook my head; agreeing.

"Oh you're faithful now my nigga?" He grinned before

answering.

"Hell yea. I don't have a choice. If I'm trying to keep my wife; I can look but not touch."

"How does it feel being married?"

"It's cool. It's no different besides your name is on a piece of paper saying you own one another." We both laughed.

"Oh shit." Miguel said as we watched Cream and the chick disappearing upstairs.

"Yo, I hope that nigga strap up. Ain't nothing like a stripper popping up with your kid nine months later." Louis said laughing as he walked over.

"I hope he knows what he's doing." Was all I said as we continued partying?

Cream

The call I got saying Monster was lurking put me in a foul mood. I tried to cover my attitude but my brother caught on and handed me a blunt.

I got dressed in some jeans, a sweater and fresh timbs. I wasn't trying to get dressed up to have a bunch of sweaty pussy around me. The only one I wanted was my wife's. Everyone came to help me celebrate but I knew some were there just for the strippers.

The clock struck twelve and the woman that stepped out the cake came over and straddled my lap. I'm not going to front, she was the only one to get my dick hard. She danced in front of me, turned around touched her ankles, then made her ass clap. I could tell she wasn't wearing any panties.

She took my hand and led me away from the crowd. I saw my cousin and brothers looking at me shaking their heads. I opened my office door, brought her inside and locked it.

She came out her heels and squatted down in front of

my dick that was now out of my jeans and in her hand, getting strokes by her perfectly manicured hands. She was so gentle and took her time making sure to please me.

"Damn, this feels good. Make me cum." She lifted her mask a little and stuck him in her mouth. I made slow love to her face as she played with her pussy through the outfit. I leaned my head back on the door and let my cum coat her throat.

"Mmmmm" She moaned. I stood her up and made her turn around taking her outfit off. Her ass was perfectly round and her tities spilled out in the front. Her pussy was shaved to perfection with no hair.

"I need to feel inside this pussy. Can I take it?" She shook her head yes. It was so wet it was making farting noises instantly. The moaning was driving me crazy as I held her leg up on the desk and dug deeper inside her.

"Fuck, this pussy wants me to make you my side chick." I felt her tense up a little.

"Don't worry. I'll keep my wife away from you." I went deeper and she started running from me. I pulled out and stuck my face in her ass and took turns going back and forth to her pussy. The orgasm she was experiencing had tears coming down. I felt them hit my shoulder as I lifted her up and fucked her against the wall.

"Can I have a kiss?"

She shook her head no; not wanting to take the mask off.

"Give me one before I fuck you harder. You already can't take it." She still wouldn't let me. I laid her on the desk, spread those legs wide and had her screaming over top of the music.

"Are you going to kiss me now?" She shook her head yes lifting the mask a little and pecking me.

"Ci Ci take it all the way off and kiss me." She smiled and kissed me aggressively while I still had her spread open.

"James I'm cumming. Baby ahhhhh..." She screamed out scratching the shit out of my back.

"I'm cumming too." Ci Ci squeezed my dick with her pussy muscles, and I shot tons of cum inside her. She wrapped her legs around my back as I laid on top of her; both trying to catch our breath.

"I love you Cecilia Thomas." She lifted my head off her chest and looked at me in my eyes.

"I love you too James Thomas. I always will." I helped her up and gave her the clothes she already had up here, which were some jeans and a sweater with some uggz.

"How did you know it was me?"

"This is your dick and it only got hard when you came over to me. None of those other chicks turned me on. Baby you did your thing though. Let me find out you can dance."

"I've been taking lessons ever since you asked me to marry you again. I've been waiting for this moment."

"Well you never cease to amaze me. I want to see more of that. Wait, should I put a pole in the bedroom?"

"If that's what you want."

"If you're going to use it, I do." I smacked her on the ass and walked her out the side door to her car.

"Baby I hope this wasn't bad luck seeing you before the wedding."

"That's superstitious stuff. We're already married

remember."

"Yea you're right."

"I'll meet you at the altar Ci Ci."

"I wouldn't miss it for the world."

"Text me when you get back to Iesha's."

"I will." I watched her pull off and went back inside. I was good now that I got my nut. She was my stress reliever and I wouldn't have it any other way.

"Please tell me you didn't fuck that stripper bro." Darius asked. Miguel and Louis stood there waiting for me to answer.

"Of course I did. Why wouldn't I fuck my wife?" Miguel spit his drink out; Darius and Louis just stared at me.

"Yo, that was Ci Ci?" Louis asked surprised.

"Yea. It was one of her wedding presents for me. You know I wasn't sleeping with no one else. Please tell me y'all weren't having nasty thoughts about my wife." They all turned their heads.

"What the fuck y'all?"

"Shit; we didn't know that was her. But dam cousin,

don't be mad. We all got some bad bitches. No disrespect cuz. We love you. We just know now why you're strung out on Ci Ci." He said making us all laugh.

"Yea alight. She'll be doing that shit in our home only."

An hour went by and the party was coming to an end. I checked my phone and noticed Ci Ci still hasn't called or text me. That wasn't like her and I was starting to get nervous.

"Yo, can one of you text your women and find out if my wife is there. I haven't heard from her since she left."

They all picked their phones up and made the call. I felt like all eyes were on me as they hung up looking at me.

"What up?" I asked putting my phone back in the clip on my hip. I saw Miguel nod and two of his bodyguards came up behind me.

"Sit down cuz."

"For what?"

Darius was walking around yelling for people to leave. Damien was standing the looking at him like he was crazy.

"Cream your wife never made it back to the house."

"WHAT??!" I tried to jump up but his bodyguards were

holding me down.

"Listen, she called Iesha and said she was on her way there. When she didn't make it back after twenty minutes, Violet, Maria and Iesha jumped in the car and went looking for her. They found the car abandoned with all her stuff still inside. The cops are with the girls now and conducting a search party." I felt the tears falling down my face and I didn't care who saw me. My wife was missing or possibly dead; you damn right I'm crying.

"I have to find her." This time I was calm when I got up, so no one touched me.

"The truck is ready." Was all the guys said as we headed out to look for her.

"Who do you think it could be?" Louis asked. Miguel was on the phone with his wife but still listening to our conversation.

"To be honest. I don't know. Monster doesn't have beef with her and we never found the person who wrote those letters." We drove to where the girls were, and Iesha and Maria were hysterical so Darius and Louis went to comfort them.

"Cream this was left in the car." Violet handed me her engagement ring with a letter.

James, I thought long and hard about our relationship and I don't think it's going to work. I'm taking my kids and leaving you. I can't bear to marry a man that cheated on me. I thought I could get past it but the more I thought about it, the more I know I couldn't. Take care and have a good life.

"There's no way she would leave me. Would she? I mean I thought we got past this Iesha. Why would she do that to me? Why would she take my kids? This can't be right. I just need to talk to her one more time. Maybe I rushed her into this." I was going on and on because I couldn't believe she would leave me like this.

"I'm sorry Cream." Iesha came over hugging me. Everyone was quiet waiting on me to speak.

"Nah, I'm not going to believe this shit. She didn't leave me. Did she?" I started walking down the dark ass street with no destination in sight. Miguel, Louis and Darius all came to my house to make sure I was ok. They stayed with me for a few days as we combed the streets looking for them.

"Do you think she really left him?" I heard my cousin ask.

"No. Somebody took her. Cream was her everything. She never would've left him or took his kids away. When he got caught cheating, she wasn't on any petty shit. She made sure he saw his son anytime he wanted. I'm telling you this entire thing is suspect if you ask me." Louis said.

"You guys don't have to stay any longer. I know she'll be back. I don't wanna keep you from your families just because mine is gone."

"Yo, go ahead with that shit. This ain't about us having families and you don't. She is still part of all of us because she's your wife."

"Thanks man." Miguel stayed a couple more weeks. Him, his wife and kids went back and promised they would be back but to call them if I heard anything. I didn't want to keep them long. He told us what his wife had just gone through with some dude named Jeremy over there. This was probably hard for her to watch. I didn't want her to have any flashbacks over it.

I started staying at my brothers' house because I couldn't sit in this house without them. I didn't hear my son running up and down the halls or Patience yelling to be picked up with her spoiled self. I missed making love to my wife and just spending time as a family. People can call me a bitch or sentimental but when a REAL NIGGA loses his family in such a way, it takes a toll on him.

I laid in bed every night praying she would call just to let me speak to the kids or even explain herself. I needed to know why she left or if that was the case. I just wanted to hear her voice and know her, and the kids were ok. I was losing hope everyday and I know others were too. I had Louis and Darius handling all my affairs.

When I went to the office just to get out the house, I could feel the stares and see the sober faces. Damien would cry with his gay ass every time he saw me. He said I reminded him of where she should be when I came in which was by my side or coming to visit.

"Boss, you know she loved you and the letter was forged." I gave him a look and asked him how he knew about the letter. He said Iesha showed it to him one day he was over there.

"Why do you think it's forged?"

"Ugh, for one... that's not her handwriting and two... you and the kids were the love of her life. Everyone knows she wouldn't have left you like this. James listen, I know y'all think because I'm gay I don't know much but I hear shit. And from what the hood is saying, she was definitely taken and it wasn't by no street niggas. The person that took her had to be planning this and watching her."

"What are you saying?"

"All I'm saying, well, all the hood is saying, is whoever did this knew what they were doing. If I were you, I would go back to the sight and see if there's any clues. Think about who she spoke to, who she got along with, anyone from her past that she didn't like? The answer is there, we just can't see it. You know they say we can't see shit even when it's staring us straight in the face."

I hated to admit it but everything he said made perfect sense. Whoever did this made her take the kids and if the letter was forged, she really didn't leave me. I went to my office and pulled up the footage, but nothing came up. There were cars everywhere so I couldn't even tell if anyone was watching her. What I did know was that whoever did this to her was going to suffer a slow death. I'm talking about almost killing the person just to allow them to get a little better and torture them over and over.

People were more than aware how I was when it came to my family. For someone to come in and feel like they could fuck with my family like that and get away with it, had another thing coming.

After I finished watching the footage and came up with nothing, I shut everything off and left out. The club was jumping tonight so I got behind the bar and helped Damien out. A few people came up giving me words of encouragement and then a few tricks trying to get my time. That's when I knew it was time to go.

I rode by Ci Ci's old house and there were lights on inside. I guess someone finally brought the property. It was a good thing because that house had some bad memories for sure.

I went by my sister in laws, went inside and passed out in the bed.

Monster

I don't know why I hooked up with this bitch; she was getting on my nerves. She picked me up from the airport earlier and had me at some house that looked familiar. The inside was really nice except for where someone spray painted *"bitches"* all over it and in certain areas was piss and shit. That bitch had the nerve to ask me help her clean it since this was the house she was going to be occupying. She lost her mind when she asked that.

I told her I was going to shower, dropped my bag off in one of the rooms that had a king size bed and a 72-inch TV. The room was nice as hell and this was the one I was staying in.

I let the hot water beat down on my skin as I picked up some shampoo to wash my dreads. I turned the shower off and walked in the room to get dressed. This bitch was laid out naked in the bed. I stared at her and she wasn't half bad looking.

She was an older woman; maybe 50, brown skin,

brown eyes and a nice set of teeth. They didn't look like dentures but now a day's, people pay top dollar to make everything look real. Her breast were at lease a C cup and perky, and her pussy had a fresh shave.

"What the hell you doing lady?" I asked. My dick was waking up at the sight of her playing with her pussy and squeezing on her nipples.

"What does it look like? Come over here and let me see what you taste like." I dropped my towel in front of her and let her take me in her mouth. I have never been one to turn down head from anyone. For her age, she was doing a hell of a job.

"Shit, that feels good." I pushed her face closer to bring my nut up. A few minutes later, I came on her face. This old hag was freaky. I couldn't even get Iesha to do that and I was with her for years.

"Can I get some of that dick?" She cocked her legs open and stuck her fingers inside. I was shocked at how wet she got.

"Fuck it, why not?" I didn't have a condom but hell her old ass wasn't getting pregnant and I doubt she had anything. It looks like she hasn't been fucked in years. I stuck my dick in and felt like I was fucking a virgin; she was so tight. I can't lie, the way she squeezed my shit made me cum right away.

"My bad. That pussy tight as hell. Give me a minute." I stroked myself to get hard again. She and I had sex for a few hours off and on. She must be on the woman Viagra because we were back at it in the morning.

"You got some good dick for a youngin."

"And you have some good pussy for an old woman." The both of us got dressed and went to lunch about an hour away.

"The plan is happening tonight."

"Ok. You never told me what we were going to do." She started telling me how she wanted to snatch Ci Ci and Iesha up. She had a score to settle with both of them. She wanted their men too but knew that would be too hard.

"You do know Cream is going to tear this city down looking for her. And Darius and Iesha may not be together but he's not going to take the shit lying down either."

"Fuck them niggas. If I get both girls, they won't matter.

I can see them suffer enough by not being able to find them."

"Ok so where are we keeping them and for how long?"

"In the house we're at. No one will look for them there. It's going to be fun having them looking all over for them and they're right under their nose." She finished explaining the plan and it sounded all good except how we were supposed to get close to either one of them.

"Leave that up to me." She said paying for the food. We went back to the house where she wrote some letter to Cream to plant in the car to make the shit look real. I just wanted to see Iesha so I can make love to her again. She claims that nigga had her heart but if he did, she would've never fucked me in the hotel.

"I just found out tonight is Cream's bachelor party and the girls are having a bachelorette party."

"Yea but how are we going to be in two places at once?" I asked her.

"We're not. When one leaves, we'll follow and go back for the other one."

"Cool. Let's go."

We sat outside some house she claims was Iesha's around nine to see if anyone would come out. It was a little after eleven when Ci Ci came out the house with a bag in her hand. She tried to keep up with her without being noticed.

By the time we realized where we were it was the guys club. She stayed in there for a few hours before her man walked her to the car. We followed her down the street and *BAM* it was just our luck the light turned red.

"GET HER NOW."

Unknown

"It's time." Was all I said and hung the phone up? It was time to get each and everyone of them back for what they did to me. I was tired of living in the shadows; watching these motherfuckers live their lives as if I didn't exist.

I was staying in some flimsy motel for a little while which is about twenty minutes away from Cream and Ci Ci. I have been doing stakeouts at their house almost every night that's how I've been able to send those two simple bitches to wreak havoc. Now that Ci Ci broke one of their noses, they backed out; talking about those bitches were too ghetto. Iesha maybe but not Ci Ci.

The day I came back, I broke into the house Ci Ci used to live in before she took her cheating ass husband back. I spray painted bitches and shit and pissed all through it. Yea it may have been nasty but so what. Why were they living in the lap of luxury and I'm in some shithole? I was going to make sure what I was going to do was something that they would never forget.

When Monster snatched Ci Ci up, she was kicking, screaming, punching and any other thing she could've done to get away. He threw her ass in the back seat and made sure the child locks were on. She kept hitting him from behind until he turned around and pointed a gun in her face. That bitch calmed down real quick.

"What do you want? Monster why are you doing this?" I forgot they were already acquainted.

"Your whack ass husband killed my sister and that nigga Darius has it coming. Come on Ci Ci you know they're no rules in this game." I snatched the ring off her finger and put it in her car with the fake ass note I left telling Cream she was leaving him.

"Who the fuck are you?" I couldn't believe the surgery worked so well she didn't have a clue who I was.

"Don't worry about it. Right now, you're going to pick up those bad ass kids and we're leaving." I had to disguise my voice because that shit sure didn't change.

"Wait! Just leave my kids. I'll do whatever you want. Please." She was pleading her life away, but it was falling on

245

deaf ears.

We left her purse, cell phone everything in her car to make it look like she was trying to get away from James quick. I knew he loved the hell out of her and his kids; shit everyone knew; so this was going to break his ass. Fuck them niggas, I could care less about their feelings. They were all about to feel my wrath; they better be ready for it. This bitch was going to suffer the most. I knew they would protect her sister like crazy and I wouldn't be able to get to her. That's ok. What I had planned Ci Ci could take for both of them.

Ci Ci

The night I danced for my husband was the last time I saw him. I was taken at a red light in the middle of the night. I knew it was bad luck to see him before the wedding, but I wanted to give him his present first.

I enjoyed the look on his face as I danced for him. We stared in each other's eyes and got lost in one another. I didn't know how he figured out it was me but I was happy because I would've left his ass for sure if he fucked a damn stripper.

I walked in the house, disarmed the alarm and told the nanny I was taking the kids with me. She said goodnight and went to bed. I wanted to call Cream so bad but my phone was in my car and she was standing right next to me with a gun. She went straight for Junior. He slept hard so he didn't realize he was being picked up. Patience woke right up when I touched her. I grabbed a few outfits for both of them, juniors iPad and charger because he couldn't live without that thing, some bottles and formula for Patience and left the house.

We got in the car and drove about fifteen minutes down

the road. The car pulled into the house I was just about to put on the market. I took junior in his old room and laid him on his bed. I got in the bed with both of them and tried to go to sleep.

I cried myself to sleep only to be awaken by them having sex down the hall. I stepped in the hallway and went to close the door to their room. I grabbed the doorknob and Monster was sitting up while the woman rode him. He looked at me licking his lips. I rolled my eyes and shut the door. There was no way in hell he would ever get a whiff of my pussy.

The next day, I was being dragged out the bed by my hair. Whoever this woman is started trying to fight me. I was beating her ass until Monster held my arms and let her get the best of me. She continued kicking me in the stomach, face, back and anywhere else her feet connected. I was crying hard because I never got to tell James I was pregnant, and I know after this beating I lost it.

"Ok, that's enough. You got your revenge for whatever she did."

"Not yet. I can't get to her sister, so she needs to take a beating for her sister too." I heard that voice before but after being kicked in the ear I thought I was bugging. I had blood coming from everywhere.

"Let go of my mommy." I heard my son screaming out.

Monster picked him up and took him downstairs. I heard my daughter crying and it was killing me that I wasn't able to get her. The woman left me lying in the hallway and went to get my daughter. Monster came upstairs and put me back in the kids' room, shut the door and I heard a click which means there was a lock on it.

The next day she made him take me to the hospital to get checked out because I had so much blood in between my legs. They told the doctors in the ER I was attacked. They also said I suffered a miscarriage, which I knew. I had some broken ribs; a broken nose, jaw and I may lose hearing in my right ear. He stayed there the entire time with me. They tried their hardest to get me to stay but the look in Monster's eyes told me to sign myself out.

I can't even tell you how long I was in this house. I saw my kids at night when it was time for bed and in the morning when they woke up. They only fed me bread and water all day.

I was being treated like an animal. I was allowed one shower a day whether I had my period or not. I always chose the night because I couldn't sleep if I was dirty.

Junior asked me every night when we were going home and if his daddy was coming to get us. I would just cry because she told me about the letter she left, telling him I didn't want to marry him. I hoped and prayed Cream didn't believe it and was out there looking for me. What I wouldn't do right now to feel him touch me or even lay with me.

****

I received a beating from this woman everyday. The days Monster wasn't around, they were worse because she would tie me up in a chair and beat the shit out of me. He would yell at her when he saw me, but it would fall on deaf ears. I think he felt bad but if he did, he should just let me go.

One-night, junior laid next to me in the bed playing on his iPad. He went to the bathroom and left his iPad on the home screen. There was a face time button. I sat up the best I could. I waited for junior to come out the bathroom to talk to him. He sat back on the bed and picked the iPad up. I felt my eyes closing from the pain medicine.

Junior turned on one of his shows and tried to get me to watch it with him. There was a TV on with his favorite Pokémon cartoon on too. He would do the same thing every day; having them both on at once.

"Junior can you turn that off for a minute." I whispered to him.

"Do you want to play on it mommy?"

"No honey. I want to see if we can call daddy on it."

"How can we call him? This is not a phone."

"Junior, I need you to press the green video camera button." He did it and the screen popped up to put a number in it.

"What's next mommy?"

"Do you remember all the times mommy taught you daddy's number?" He shook his head yes.

"I need you to put daddy's number in that line right there." I pointed and he did it. My baby remembered the number with no problem. I looked for a send button and I pointed to it but felt my self-falling asleep.

"We can call him tomorrow junior." Was the last thing I remember saying.

I didn't see my kids for a few days or weeks after that night. She said I looked pitiful and was unfit to take care of my kids. I couldn't yell or scream to keep her from taking them out the room. Monster came in the room one day when she was out to talk to me.

"Where's your sister?" He asked smoking a blunt. The smell had me gagging.

"Monster why are you letting her do this to me? I never did anything to you."

"Yea, but your man did. A life for a life." At that moment, I knew they had plans on killing me. I let the tears fall and didn't care about anything but my kids from this point.

"I don't understand."

"That detective that was fucking your man was my sister." I covered my mouth in shock. James told me he killed her but he never told me she was his sister.

"I didn't know she was your sister, but I can't say I'm upset. She put a gun in my face because she was in her feelings

252

over my husband." He blew smoke in the air staring at me.

"Yea, she was on some petty shit but he didn't have to kill her." He looked like he was in deep thought sitting there.

"Why are you letting her beat on me? And she's doing it in front of my kids."

"I know. I told her about that shit but she has some personal vendetta against you and your sister."

"You would allow her to do this to Iesha?"

"Hell no." I would beat her ass if she laid a finger on Iesha.

"Ok, so why would you allow her to do it to me?"

"I never fucked you. Iesha is my girl and the shit your man did makes me not give a fuck. I'm sorry but I can't help you with that."

"That's foul. I've always been cool with you."

"So you're telling me if you saw your man whooping my ass, you would stop him because I used to date your sister?" I put my head down.

"Exactly."

"Just do me a favor then."

253

"What?" He put the blunt out on the bottom of his boot.

"Can you make sure my kids get back to him once she kills me? I want them to be with one of us." I wiped my eyes and got up slowly to use the bathroom. I came out and he was still sitting there.

"Look, all I can do is ask her to stop with the beatings. I can't promise anything, but I need you to tell me where your sister is."

"Why do you want her?"

"Because she is about to run away with me."

"You do know she has five kids right?"

"Damn, how did she get that many?"

"She had a set of twins and Sky disappeared and left her daughter, so Iesha is raising her."

"That's ok we can take all them fuckers with us. I'll be their daddy."

"What the fuck is this?" The woman walked in staring at us like she caught us doing something. She stepped closer to me and smacked me so hard one of my teeth flew out on the side of my mouth.

"Yo, cut that shit out." He yelled snatching her out the room.

"What you fucking her too?" I could hear her questioning him in the hallway.

"No. I'm in love with her sister but if you keep beating on her, I'm not going to be fucking you either."

I heard them downstairs and the door closed. I could hear footsteps coming up the steps, so I laid in the bed to act like I was on my way to sleep. It didn't matter she came in with something in her hand. But when I looked, it was a cast iron skillet and all I saw was black.

"Mommy wake up. I'm calling daddy to come get us." I heard junior in my ear. I opened my eyes and saw him on the iPad. I saw the number dial and I heard him answer.

"Daddy." James didn't answer

"Daddy." He still didn't answer. I saw the frustration in my sons face. I told him to dial it again. He did and tried calling back. I started fading in and out again. I saw the phone going and that's when I realized Junior was pressing the mute button.

Iesha

Four months had gone by and we still had no luck finding my sister. Hell, she didn't even contact me. My kids miss seeing her and their cousins just like I do.

I've been trying to keep myself busy to distract myself and it works until Cream shows up. He is a complete mess and in total denial that she would leave him and I agree. She was ecstatic to be marrying him and after she performed for him at his bachelor party and they had sex, there's no way she left. There was some foul play involved and the sooner we found out the better.

Cream has been staying with us since Ci Ci's been gone and that's fine because the kids love spending time with their uncle. He loves playing with them, but you can tell he misses his kids too. He and I have gone back to the spot her car was found thinking we'll find something, but we never do.

"Hey sis. What's for dinner?" He kissed my cheek and sat at the table.

"I was in the mood for seafood so we're having shrimp scampi, but I made some lobster tails too. There's a salad in the fridge and baked potatoes in the oven."

"Damn that sounds good." Darius said walking in. He pecked me on the lips and sat down with us. We tried not to show too much affection in front of him. We didn't want to rub it in his face. Creams phone rang so Darius and I kept talking.

"Hello. Yo who the fuck is this?" He yelled in the phone. He said hello a few more times and hung up.

"What's up bro?" Darius turned to him.

"Nothing. I've been getting these phone calls lately where the person doesn't say shit. But keeps calling back."

"Then get the number changed." I thought he was going to kill Darius just off the way he looked at him.

"Are you crazy? What if Ci Ci tries to reach me?"

"A'ight man damn. She has our number too." Darius put his hands up.

"My bad man. I'm just stressed the fuck out. I'm going to take a plate and lay down. Tell the kids I'll play with them tomorrow." We heard him shut the door.

"Baby maybe we should get your mom over here to talk to him."

"Why you say that?"

"Darius that is a broken man. He knows his wife wouldn't just leave him but he has no way to find her. She just disappeared without a trace and that shit just don't happen to black people."

"Black people? Really Iesha?"

"I'm serious. You see that shit on the news about white people all the time. You think I'm crazy but Ci Ci didn't leave him and I think someone has her I just don't know who."

"What about those bitches from the mall?" He asked me.

"I doubt those two idiots even know how to kidnap a mouse. Whoever did this, planned it and were waiting for the right time. The question now is who would want to make sure she left him for good? Who benefitted from it?"

Darius and I fed the kids and bathed them. They wanted to watch Kung Fu Panda as a family. I sent Summer and Lyric to knock on Cream's door since they were the oldest.

"Uncle Cream can you watch this movie with us?" He came out giving us the evil eye. We knew he wouldn't tell the kids no that's why we sent them. He needed to come out the room for some fresh air anyway. His phone rang again, and he went to answer it.

"This is the same number. Just listen." The kids weren't paying us any mind.

"Hello." He put it on speaker. You could hear something rattling in the background.

"That's J.J." Summer said lying on her stomach watching TV. We all looked at her like she was crazy as the person was still on the phone. She called James Jr. J.J. when I had my son because she said it was too many juniors.

"Summer come here honey." Cream called to her. She rolled over and got up slowly because she was into the movie.

"Baby how do you know that's JJ?"

"That's Pokémon music in the background. That's his favorite show playing on the background. You don't hear it?" He said he heard noise a few times but never paid attention to the music.

"James Jr is that you?" The phone went dead. He gave Summer a big hug and went to get dressed. He came out and his phone rang again.

"Hello."

"Daddy." I saw the tears coming down Creams face.

"Junior where are you?"

"Daddy, mommy's not waking up."

"Junior what's wrong with mommy?" Cream was pacing back and forth in the kitchen. We stepped out the living room so the kids wouldn't hear and get upset.

"She has red stuff coming out her ears and nose."

"Junior put the phone to mommy's ear."

"Daddy, I don't have a phone. I have an iPad." How was he calling me with an iPad? I would figure that out later.

"Ok son. Put the iPad to her ear." You could hear rustling in the background.

"Ci Ci baby, it's your husband. Baby, I need you to listen to my voice and tell me where you are." I was crying so hard, Darius had to hug me to keep me calm.

"Ci Ci please. I need you to find your strength to just

tell me where you are?"

"James." I heard just above a whisper.

"Yes baby. I'm coming to get you; where are you?"

"James come get the kids."

"Ok baby. I need you to tell me where you are."

"James, I lost the baby." I gasped and covered my
mouth. The look on his face was scary.

"What baby? Never mind. We can talk about that later.
One more time baby, where are you?"

"Home."

"Home." We all said at the same time.

"Daddy, mommy went to sleep. When are you coming
to get us? Grandma keeps hitting mommy and the monster man
doesn't like to hear my sister cry."

All our mouths hung to the ground.

TO BE CONTINUED......

CPSIA information can be obtained
at www.ICGtesting.com
Printed in the USA
LVHW041625130819
627493LV00003B/362/P

9 781074 104306